Edged

Marie Tuhart

https://www.marietuhart.com/

QUALITY CONTROL: We strive to produce error-free books, but even with all the eyes that see the story during the production process, slips get by. So please, if you find a typo or any formatting issues, please let us know at marie@marietuhart.com so that we may correct it.

Thank you!

EDGED

Wicked Sanctuary: Surrender your inhibitions.

He has an artist's passion.

She can't let anyone in.

Two lovers learning commitment doesn't mean losing themselves.

Kaley Clark's job as a dog groomer is perfect for her, right up until she arrives at her favorite client's house and the woman's grandson opens the door. Kaley recognizes him immediately. The man was a cutting-edge artist and she couldn't help being attracted to him.

Coming off the high of his first gallery showing, Anthony Payne just wants to paint until he sees Kaley. She is the perfect model. He's captivated by her and is willing to do anything to get her into his life.

When a trauma from her past comes between them, can Kaley learn to trust Anthony with her body and her heart?

ACKNOWLEGMENTS

There are several people I want to thank for supporting me through this book:

Laurie, thank you for all your support and writing sessions.

Red Quill Editing team, you are the best team to work with. You can always make me laugh.

Publisher's Note: This book contains a dominant male, spunky heroine, sexy situations, trauma around mugging and adoption.

To My Readers:

This book contains elements of the BDSM lifestyle that are only true to life in this book. There are various relationship dynamics in the lifestyle, which are decided between the people involved. While I have researched and talked with people in the lifestyle, this is my take on how my characters choose to live.

If you decide to explore the lifestyle yourself, please remember to always be safe. Never go home with someone you don't know. Attend a munch or a small get-together first to see if this is something you want in your life. Reading and living are very different.

FYI: Anthony was introduced in *Power Play*, Rose and Oliver in *Claiming Rose*. You don't have to read these novellas in order to enjoy *Edged*.

Enjoy.

Chapter 1

Kaley Clark drove her Fluff and Puff van down the road, proud of the professional yet friendly look of the logo painted on both sides. Impish dogs and sly cats and her contact information—the perfect advertisement of the business she'd started a few years ago and needed to thrive.

She parked in the circular driveway of the ranch style house, surprised not to see her client, Clara Pierce, waiting at the door to welcome people to her home. She hoped Clara was okay.

Securing her shoulder-length auburn hair, Kaley pulled her equipment out of the van, made her way up the front stairs, and rang the bell. Nugget, Clara's Maltipoo, barked. The door opened and… Kaley took a step back.

Anthony, or Payne as they called him in the club, stood there, his black hair mussed, and his blue eyes dazed. "Can I help you?" His deep voice sent shivers up her spine.

"I'm—"

A voice Kaley knew well came from behind the man she couldn't take her eyes off. "It's Kaley, let her in, Anthony. Remember? She's here to groom Nugget."

"You're the dog groomer?"

Kaley bit the inside of her lower lip, hoping her heart would resume a normal rhythm. She'd watched Anthony from afar, intoxicated by his powerful shoulders and piercing eyes. His intensity both excited and intimidated her. "People have trouble believing I'm the dog groomer." She glanced down at her apron with her logo on it. "I don't know why."

"Maybe because you'd make the perfect model for painting," he said, his gaze roving from Kaley's head to her toes and back again. She warmed at the appreciative look in his dark eyes. "My apologies," Anthony said, stepping back. "Come in." He reached for her folded up grooming table. "Here, let me take that."

"I'm fine." She shifted past him.

Clara's voice rang out strong and clear. "I'm in the family room, dear. Don't let my grandson take you off guard."

"Is she okay?" Kaley asked in a low voice.

"Sprained ankle. She's been told to stay off it." He shut the door as Kaley walked down the small hallway.

Nugget started whining and wiggling when she saw Kaley. "Hi, Clara." The woman was sitting with her leg propped up on a pillow, trying to hold the energetic dog.

"Allow me," Anthony said, maneuvering around her to remove the baby gate across the doorway. "We're trying to keep Nugget confined to this room so Gran doesn't go running after him."

"I see." Kaley slipped by him and smelled paint and turpentine. She'd heard Anthony was an artist, and his comment when she first arrived backed that up. Did he paint his models clothed or nude? Her body heated at the thought of being painted by him in the nude. Not that it was going to happen, but she could fantasize.

Nugget leaped out of Clara's arms and launched herself at Kaley. "Easy, Nugget." Kaley set her stuff down and caught the dog as she jumped into her arms. Laughter bubbled up as doggy kisses covered her face.

"Nugget," Clara admonished.

"It's fine," Kaley said, tightening her arms around Nugget so the small dog didn't fall. "Are you in pain, Clara? I could have done this on another day."

"It's nothing." Clara waved her hands. "Doctor's being cautious."

"Doctor is making sure you heal," Anthony said, giving Clara a pointed look.

Kaley's knees weakened. There it was, that Dom stare. Oh yes, she'd seen him around Wicked Sanctuary, and she'd kept her distance. The man oozed power that made her apprehensive, but that didn't stop her lady bits from sitting up and taking notice.

"The usual?" she asked Clara. She was here to groom the dog, not make eyes at Anthony. No matter what her body said.

"Oh yes, dear. That would be wonderful."

"All right. Let me go set up in the laundry room, and I'll come back for Nugget." Kaley turned.

"Do you need help with anything?" Anthony asked as he cupped her elbow.

Tingles flowed from her elbow throughout her body. She didn't want to react to him this way but couldn't seem to control herself.

"I'll be fine." She watched him remove another baby gate and walked into the laundry room. Kaley was aware of Anthony watching her while she set up. Her skin prickled with…it wasn't exactly excitement, but it wasn't dislike either. In fact, it felt quite dangerous, something Kaley tried to steer well clear of.

"Come here, Nugget," Anthony called, and the dog came running into the laundry room. Did everyone follow the man's orders? Kaley picked the dog up and put him into the sink and began bathing him.

"Maybe when you're done with Nugget we can talk?" Anthony asked.

She worked the shampoo into the dog's coat. "Talk?" Now she sounded like a parrot. "I'm not sure we have anything to talk about."

"I think we might." His voice was strong, and the words warmed her like hot chocolate on a cold day.

Kaley didn't answer, but damn if her insides didn't melt at the sound of his voice. Instead, she rinsed off Nugget, wrapped him in a towel, and placed him on the grooming table.

Anthony sighed, then left, and she blew out a breath. While she might have seen Anthony at the club, she doubted very much he knew who she was, and it was better that way. His kink was not her kink.

Besides, she wasn't looking for a Dom, just someplace she could relax, be herself, and make some friends. She was still exploring the lifestyle.

Nugget licked her hand, and Kaley laughed. "Thank you for the kiss." Leave it to the dog to get her attention where it needed to be.

* * * *

Anthony Payne watched the pretty dog groomer give Nugget a bath. Fluff and Puff. He grinned as he as he walked away. Kaley seemed familiar to him. He didn't recognize her business name. Could he have met her around town?

Maybe at his gallery opening a few weeks ago. The opening had been filled with people, and as much as he didn't like crowds, Dane had convinced him that he had to keep up appearances. "How long will the grooming take?" he asked his grandmother.

"About an hour." Clara picked up her book.

"Okay, I'm going to go back and paint for a bit."

"Go."

He made his way to the sunroom that had become his temporary workspace after Gran sprained her ankle. The doctor said she needed to stay off it until it healed, which could be two weeks.

Anthony had immediately moved in. Not that he lived far away. There was a cottage on Gran's property he'd lived in since he was eighteen, when his parents threw him out. He shook his head.

He didn't want to think about his parents or that time in his life. He'd been a confused young adult they'd set adrift. Luckily, Gran took him in. He stepped into the sunroom and put a new canvas on the stand.

Then he remembered where he'd seen Kaley. Wicked Sanctuary. She worked behind the bar, and he'd tried sketching her a few times after he left the club, but he never could seem to get her essence. Seeing her today he knew why.

Up close and personal was what he needed. She'd stirred up his muse. He wanted to bring his vision of Kaley to life. Hell, he wanted to paint her. That would be the only way to appease his muse.

Once she was done with Nugget, he'd talk with her about allowing him to paint her. It was more than his muse being intrigued with her. His dick had leaped to attention when he saw her. Thankfully, his clothing hid his unusual reaction to her.

Had that happened at the club? He would have remembered if it had, wouldn't he? Picking up a piece of charcoal, he began to sketch. First a chaise lounge, then Kaley lying upon it. She was going to be his new inspiration.

* * * *

"Excuse me." A female voice close to his ear and her soft touch on his shoulder caused him to jump. "Sorry I startled you; I've been saying your name for what feels like five minutes."

Anthony blinked at Kaley. Sometimes he got so caught up in his work he'd lose track of time. "It's okay." He checked where she was standing. Thank goodness his body blocked most of his sketch. He wasn't ready to share it with anyone yet.

"Your grandmother wanted you, and I'm getting ready to leave."

"Already?" He rubbed the back of his neck.

Kaley smiled. "It's been over an hour. Nugget is all clean and groomed, and I had a nice visit with your grandmother for a few minutes."

"Anthony," his grandmother called.

"Be right there." He turned and shifted the easel, then glanced over at Kaley. "I'd like to paint you." How unlike him to blurt that out.

Her light green eyes grew wide. "Paint me?" She started to shake her head, then glanced around. "Oh my goodness. This is a beautiful room."

Anthony smiled. "I could paint you in here where you could look out the skylight and let your mind float."

For a second her shoulders relaxed, then she stiffened. "I can't."

"Please." Anthony tried and failed to hold back the pleading tone. He'd heard the legends of an artist's near compulsion to capture a subject on canvas; now he understood it was real. And he was sure he'd do whatever she asked if she would agree.

"I don't think so." She walked to the doorway. "I barely have time for anything outside of work. Sorry."

"I won't take a lot of your time." Anthony strode over to her.

"No. Sorry." Kaley walked away, and his shoulders dropped with discouragement. Then a silly grin spread across his face. He'd find a way to get her to agree to sit for him. He wasn't going to let her go that easily.

* * * *

Kaley forced herself to breathe normally. How could she explain it? Anthony painting was like watching a master at work. He hadn't even realized she was there. And the room he was painting in…

The domed glass ceiling in the old fashioned sunroom bathed the room in perfect light. But it wasn't just that. She could sit in that room for hours just gazing up at the sky or even reading a book. She shook her head as a wave of sadness washed over her.

She didn't have time for such flights of fancy. She had a business to run and no time to sit for Anthony to paint her. Why did he want to paint her anyway? She wasn't model beautiful. Getting closer to Anthony, even just for a painting, could be trouble. That was something she didn't need in her life. She'd had enough excitement over the years.

"I'm going now, Clara."

"Thank you, dear, for everything."

"Sure." Kaley gave Nugget ear scratches before she made her way out of the house. Anthony stood in the doorway of the sunroom, and she felt the heat of his gaze on her back. Thank goodness she'd already taken her equipment out to the van. He'd probably be right there to help her, and if she spent much more time in his presence, she'd cave. Time to get to her next appointment.

She climbed into her van but couldn't resist looking at the house. Anthony stood framed in the front door, his dark hair slightly mussed and the shadow of a beard that made her want to run her hands along his chin. Her gut clenched. All that male attention was focused on her.

Was that a bad thing? Yes. She didn't have time for men, and Anthony wasn't the right man for her. For one thing, she didn't do his kind of kink. Plus, maybe she was being judgmental, but she was pretty sure he'd grown up with wealth and privilege. She was just a poor kid from the wrong side of the tracks. It was better this way.

Kaley pulled out of the driveway, feeling disappointed she couldn't stay longer and watch Anthony work. Where was all this coming from? She'd seen Anthony at the club and hadn't had this reaction to him. What made today so different?

Maybe it was seeing him outside of Wicked Sanctuary. There the men seemed so dominant and overwhelming. Today she saw a man taking care of his grandmother, and it warmed her heart.

And just because she hadn't seen him with Clara before didn't mean anything. What difference did it make? Anthony wasn't for her. The last thing she wanted was a man in her life who could become special to her.

Chapter 2

Kaley walked into the Double D BBQ at seven and smiled when she saw her friend Dani.

"I'm so glad you could make it," Dani said, giving her a hug.

"Me too." Dani had taken her under her wing at Wicked Sanctuary since Kaley was a brand-new sub. Dani was actually the one who told Kaley about Wicked Sanctuary when the two hit it off while Kaley was grooming a dog at the same house where Dani landscaped.

They sat and ordered food. "So how did today go for you?" Dani asked.

"Busy, but okay." Kaley glanced around. "I might need some advice."

"Oh?" Dani's brown eyes twinkled.

"Yes." Kaley swallowed. "I saw Anthony."

Dani sat up straighter. "Where?"

"I groom his grandmother's dog. He was there helping her out because she sprained her ankle."

"To have a man take care of his grandmother. What a treasure."

"Dani, the house is gorgeous. It's obvious he comes from old money." Dani was one of the few people she'd confided in about her background. Oh, and there was Max, the owner of Wicked Sanctuary, but that was because Max allowed her to work behind the bar to cover her yearly dues.

"Kaley, stop getting hung up about how you grew up."

"I can't help it." Whenever she was out and about, she worried about running into someone who knew her when she was younger. Her home life hadn't been the best.

"From what you told me, you did everything you could to get yourself out of that situation. Heck, you even took a bartending job at the club when both your parents were alcoholics."

"Only because Max doesn't allow alcohol. He understands at any event where he does allow alcohol, I can't bartend." And she wouldn't. Not growing up with parents who cared more about their next drink than making sure their children were fed, clothed, and taken care of.

"Right. But tell me more about meeting Anthony. Did he recognize you?"

"I don't think so." Kaley thought back. Maybe there had been a flash of recognition, but it was gone in a second.

"Not unusual, you've only been at the club a few times when he's there."

"Are all the Doms so…overwhelming?"

Dani laughed. "Most are. Anthony can be particularly intense. Besides, his skill with words can create a great mind fuck. He's the knife play expert."

Kaley's mouth dropped open. She knew about his skill at saying things that messed with a person's head, but the knives? Her hand covered her abdomen. "Knives," she whispered. A sliver of pain swept over her skin and disappeared in an instant.

"You've gone pale. Are you okay?"

She wanted to say yes but couldn't. Memories nearly overwhelmed her until she was pulled back to the present when the waiter brought their food.

"I'm starving," she said, trying to cover up her reaction. No one knew about that, not even Dani.

Dani kept her gaze on Kaley for a moment before looking at her food. "Let's eat, but I want to know more."

"What more is there to tell?" Kaley picked up her brisket sandwich.

"There's always more."

They finished eating, paid the check, and decided to go for a walk. "So, tell me more about you and Anthony," Dani said.

"There's nothing more. We chatted, I groomed Nugget and went on my way."

"That blush on your cheeks tells me there was more to it."

Kaley sighed. She wanted Dani's advice, but that meant she had to tell her. There was no harm in that. "Anthony asked me to model for him."

Dani squealed. "Are you going to do it?"

"No."

"Why not?"

"Come on, Dani. I know we've only known each other a short time, but I'm not model material."

"Bull. You've got wonderful cheekbones, and your eyes sparkle when you let yourself be happy."

Kaley tilted her head. "You make me sound like a beauty queen or something."

"Quit being so hard on yourself." Dani stopped in front of The Morgan Gallery. "Come on, let's go in." Before Kaley could say a word, Dani took her by the arm and pulled her into the gallery.

Kaley hadn't been inside the gallery before. She almost laughed; the last time she'd been around art like this was a school field trip to the Seattle Art Museum when she was younger. She moved past the abstract paintings and...oh goodness.

This art was erotic, or did they call it fetish? She wasn't sure. All she knew was it was explicit. She stared at the first painting of a menage with two men and a woman, whose face radiated her immense enjoyment.

The next painting was a man in a jock strap with a harness on. He looked hard and tough. In the next panel, a male hand caressed the woman's lower back, and Kaley instantly noticed the softening of the subject's features.

Her breath caught as she moved to the next painting. A female submissive tied to a spanking bench, her ass red, her Dom standing next to her with a flogger in one hand and the other hand resting on her back. The sheer love shining from the woman's eyes made Kaley jealous.

A man had never made her feel that way. Oh, she'd dated, but the men always seemed so shallow or intent on sex. Or so hesitant she was left to make the decisions on where they went and what they did. Kaley didn't want that, and it was one of the reasons she went to Wicked Sanctuary. There, she could let go of her control and be herself, but only to a point.

When she thought about it, her issues stemmed from her childhood where she'd had no control. She *still* carried that small, scared child inside her. She sighed. Maybe one day she'd find a man willing to help her explore on her terms.

"I see you found Anthony's art," Dani said.

"Anthony did these?" Kaley's admiration for him increased. How would he make her look if he painted her? "He's very talented."

"He is. This is the first time his work has been shown in a gallery."

"Why? It's beautiful." Kaley could see the loving lines of the strokes. He didn't sexualize the concept, but allowed the sensuality of the figures to come out without being overt. It was open and honest.

"You know as well as I do how judgmental people can be. This is sensual, fetish art."

Heat invaded Kaley's cheeks. Thinking back to dinner, hadn't she been judgmental earlier with saying Anthony had money. But this…these were works of art. Nothing people wouldn't see in any museum in the world. Nude sculptures were found in almost any museum.

"You brought me in here on purpose."

"Guilty. I wanted you to see what Anthony creates."

Kaley had to admit that Dani was right. She needed to see Anthony's work. Not that she was going to pose for him, but she now understood him a little better. He might be a Dom, but his portrayals of the women in the painting showed he saw more than most people did. He revealed buried pain being set free, along with contentment, caring, love. And he brought out the sensuality of his subjects.

Curious, she glanced at one of the price tags. Holy shit! She wasn't going to take back her words about his wealth. This one painting cost almost a year of her gross business income.

"Come on." Dani looped her arm through Kaley's. "You wanted to be home by nine, and it's after eight-thirty now."

"Thanks."

Together, they walked to Kaley's apartment. Gabriel, Dani's fiancé, was waiting when they got there. He'd dropped Dani at the restaurant and offered to pick them up, but they wanted to walk. He greeted Kaley, then helped Dani into their vehicle. Kaley waved to them as she stepped inside her apartment building.

Maybe one day she'd find a good man like Gabriel.

Chapter 3

Kaley slipped behind the bar at Wicked Sanctuary at seven-thirty Saturday night. She took a deep breath and let it out. Her muscles relaxed. She wondered if Anthony would be here tonight because she couldn't get his paintings out of her head. Maybe if she saw him again in the club with a sub, it would help dismiss her wanton thoughts.

"Evening, Kaley. How are you?" Max asked.

"I'm fine, Master Max."

He nodded. "I'm assuming Noah drove you?"

"Yes, Sir." Kaley only had her business van, and it was too distinctive to drive to Wicked Sanctuary, so she usually caught a ride with Noah or one of the subs.

"And who is taking you home?"

"Probably Oliver and Rose." Most women might be upset at his questions, but Kaley understood Max was only looking out for her, like he did all the subs in the club.

"All right, if something doesn't work out, let me know."

"Of course, Sir." Max left, and Kaley grinned. She didn't mind Max's protectiveness; it felt good after being the one to make sure she and her siblings were safe when they were growing up.

Kaley checked supplies out of habit, but the bar had been restocked, so there was plenty of water, soda, and juice. The smell of beef and fresh cooked dough hit her senses, and she looked up.

Lara was here with Colby, and they were setting up the food. Oh good. She'd rushed home from her last job, took a quick shower, and changed before Noah picked her up, and she hadn't been able to eat. She'd have to wait a while before she could grab anything, but she'd survive.

"Go."

Kaley turned to see Noah. "What?"

"Go get some food. I heard your stomach growling for most of the drive."

Embarrassment heated her skin. "Sorry."

"Hey." Noah cupped her chin. "I would have stopped and made you eat something, but we were running late. Go. I can watch the bar."

"But…"

Noah placed his fingers against her lips. "Go, Kaley."

That low Dom voice shot vibrations over her spine. "Yes, Sir."

She slipped around Noah and over to the food table. "Hi, Kaley," Lara said.

"Hi, Lara. Everything smells heavenly."

"Fill your plate. I know you work behind the bar so get it now. And if you need something later, flag me down, and I'll bring you more."

"Thank you." Kaley still had trouble accepting how open and helpful everyone at Wicked Sanctuary was. She filled her plate with empanadas, a bagel dog, a spring roll, veggie samosas, and two brownie bars. That should tide her over.

Kaley returned to the bar and set her plate out of the way but couldn't resist biting into one of the empanadas. The beef melted in her mouth, and she closed her eyes. A chuckle had her opening her eyes. Noah stood there watching her.

"Do I need to take you in hand to make sure you eat more often?"

"I'm good, Sir. I was running late today."

"Almost every week," he said. "I may have only been your trainer, but I'm still watching out for you no matter what. So promise me you'll eat regular meals?"

Kaley's heart warmed. "I promise. As I said, today was just one of those days."

"All right. I'll relieve you at eleven."

"Okay."

Noah nodded and walked away. Kaley sighed. She was tired, but tonight she might stay a little later than usual. She didn't want to cut Oliver and Rose's time in the club short; most nights they were ready to leave by midnight at the latest. She wanted to sit and watch everyone tonight so she would feel more comfortable.

She'd finished her classes only two months ago; maybe staying later would help her relax a bit and take her mind off her work and everything she had to do tomorrow on her one day off.

* * * *

Anthony strode into Wicked Sanctuary, trying to cope with his failure to reach Kaley. He'd searched for her information online and found her business website. He'd emailed her, and she replied—again—she wasn't interested in him painting her.

Next, he left her a voicemail. She texted him that she wasn't going to change her mind. Failure didn't sit well with him, especially since he couldn't get her to even agree to see him to chat. The woman had him tied in knots, and he was without a knife to cut them.

"Hey, Payne," Noah said.

Anthony grinned and shook his friend's hand. Several of the members called him *Payne* as a joke since he liked to play with knives, and when he turned eighteen, he started using his biological parents' last name. "Noah, what's going on tonight?"

"Not much. It's pretty quiet tonight for a Saturday."

"Unusual?" While he'd been a club member for a while, he wasn't very familiar with how busy they were or weren't.

"A bit, but it might be the time of year. We're going into fall, and the kids have gone back to school. Parents are spending more time with school prep and sports."

Anthony had never thought about that. "I'm going to go hang out at the bar, want to join me?"

"Working the floor right now, but maybe later."

Anthony nodded and made his way to the bar. He froze when he saw Kaley. His mood lightened. Maybe he could chat her up tonight and show her he wasn't such a bad guy. Anthony slipped onto one of the stools and waited. Kaley was busy at the other end of the bar.

Her auburn hair was braided, extending down her back but exposing her neck and creamy skin. When she agreed to allow him to paint her, he'd make sure her hair was down, cascading over her shoulders.

His gaze caught on the bright red sports bra and black boy shorts. No. He wanted to paint her in the nude, but it was way too soon for that.

Kaley turned, and he saw her profile and frowned. Her face looked too thin from this angle. Was she not eating properly? If she became his, he would make sure she ate. Where in the hell did that thought come from? He wanted to paint her; he was not planning to take her on as a sub.

Although the idea had merits. He glanced at her wrist. White wristband: she was available. Another thing to think about. He kept his gaze on her as she moved down the bar, serving patrons.

She stopped in front of him, and her eyes went wide. "Good evening, what can I get you?"

Her voice was calm, but he noticed she didn't say Sir. Had she forgotten the protocols in the club? Possibly she was new. He'd fix that. "Soda, please."

Kaley reached down and pulled out four cans and set them in front of him. Interesting she didn't just ask him. He chose his favorite, and she put the others away. She placed a tall glass with ice in front of him, snapped open the can, and emptied it into the glass.

"Thank you." He took a sip. "How long have you been working the bar?"

"About a month now."

"Sir."

She blinked, then said, "Yes, Sir."

Damned if that 'Yes Sir' didn't make his cock twitch even if it was part of the club protocol. "I don't remember seeing you last night."

"Only on Saturday nights. I do have another job." She turned her head as another patron sat down. "Excuse me, Sir."

Anthony kept his gaze on her as she served drinks to other members and handed off several bottles of water to one of the subs.

He called her name softly when she walked by him. "Kaley."

"Yes, Sir?"

"Talk with me."

"I need to work, Sir."

"You can do that, but I'd like to chat while you're not busy." He saw hesitation flash in her eyes. "I promise to let you do your job."

"And no talking about me modeling for you, Sir?"

"You drive a hard bargain." He liked the flash of fire in her. A woman who knew her own mind. He wanted to know why she wouldn't pose for him. He needed to understand.

"Take it or leave it, Sir." She crossed her arms over her chest.

"While I'm sitting here at the bar I won't mention it."

She nodded and went to fill another drink. Anthony was glad he'd come to Wicked Sanctuary tonight. Now maybe he could find out what made Kaley tick.

* * * *

Kaley wasn't sure what to make of Anthony sitting at the bar. When she wasn't serving others, she stood and chatted with him. True to his word, he didn't mention her sitting for him. It was actually nice to have someone to talk to.

The bar wasn't super busy tonight, and it staved off boredom. She was surprised when Noah joined them.

"My turn," Noah said.

"Is it eleven already, Sir?"

"Yes. Go relax." Noah gave her a little slap on the butt.

"Behave, Sir." She walked out from behind the bar to find Anthony waiting for her with a frown on his face.

"Do you want me to talk to Noah?"

"What?"

"He slapped your ass."

Kaley laughed. "Noah was my instructor during my classes. It was nothing serious… Sir." She needed to remember to use Sir. Damned pesky club protocols again.

Anthony inclined his head. "As long as he has consent." He held out his arm. "Would you sit with me and talk more?"

She hesitated. Not because she didn't enjoy chatting with Anthony, but she wanted to be ready when Oliver and Rose wanted to go home. Interesting, she was thinking of sitting with Anthony and talking. He was so easy to talk to, and some of the loneliness inside her disappeared when she was with him.

Kaley let herself really look at Anthony. Like most the Doms in the club, he wore black pants and loafers, but he was in a black t-shirt instead of bare chested. She wondered about that.

"All right." Decision made, she put her hand on his outstretched arm. His strong muscles flexed, and his skin was warm to the touch. Her fingers tingled with the contact. What was going on with her body? It wasn't like her to react to a simple touch.

"Thank you." His hand covered hers, and he led her across the club to one of the quieter areas. He waited until she was seated on the love seat before joining her.

Once beside her, he picked up her hand and fingered her white wristband. "How new are you?"

"My classes ended a month ago, so fairly new, Sir." It wasn't an unusual question; several of the Doms had asked her the same. And when invited her to play, they were gracious when she turned them down. She was still getting the feel of Wicked Sanctuary and wasn't ready to play in public.

He nodded. "Would you be interested in sceneing with me?"

"I'm not sure, Sir." That wasn't the automatic no she'd given to other Doms, and she filed that away to think about later. "You've not asked me before tonight."

"I'm an idiot, pure and simple. I guess I was so busy checking out the club, I barely looked at the bar. I should have." He threaded his fingers with hers. "And let's drop the Sir for now."

She nodded as she ground her teeth together to hide her hurt at not being a noticeable kind of girl. "So, you didn't know who I was at your grandmother's?" She was curious about that.

"It took me a little bit to remember where I'd seen you." His blue gaze never left her face. "You recognized me?"

"I did. I saw you a few weeks ago when you gave a demo." She shivered.

"It scared you."

"Yes." She lifted her chin. Kaley was tired of people judging her by her fears.

"No worries." He rubbed the back of her hand with his thumb in a soothing motion, and Kaley began to relax. "That's too advanced for you right now. What do you like?"

"Wouldn't it be easier to get my information from Master Max?" She was aware that several of the Doms had read her questionnaire before they approached her.

"For some, but I'd rather discuss these things with you."

Kaley nodded and shifted. How did she feel about sceneing with Anthony? Her blood heated. Other Doms hadn't affected her like this. Usually, there was no reaction to a Dom asking her if she wanted to play, but not with him. Her lady parts lit up like a Christmas tree.

With Master Max and a couple of the other long-time Doms, she was intimidated. She knew that wasn't their intention, but their demeanor made her shrink into herself. A Dom voice was one thing; anything more and the fear crept into her throat.

Noah was kind and gentle during training; even so, Kaley wasn't a proper sub and probably never would be. That bothered her, but what could she do about it? Being here felt right. And the nervous excitement she felt at Anthony's touch and questions made her wonder if she could become the right kind of sub. If she could let go of all the burdens life had thrown at her and just…be.

"What would you like to know?" she asked.

"How much do you know about the lifestyle?"

Kaley tilted her head. "The classes helped me learn a lot more than I knew before, which wasn't a lot."

"Why did you join?"

"Good question." Kaley shifted in her position. Anthony still held her hand, and she enjoyed the feel of his skin against hers. "I was looking for a place to belong."

"You could have joined a book club or any other public group. Dig deeper for me."

She took a deep breath. "I wanted a place where I wasn't judged on my appearance or lack of money. I wanted to be accepted for who I was."

"May I?" Anthony lifted his free hand. "I'd like to do more than hold your hand."

"Okay."

He ran his fingers over her cheek before curving them around the back of her neck. Her nerves awakened at his touch. His hand kneaded tight muscles, and like magic, she relaxed.

"No one should ever make you feel unacceptable. If they do, it's their failure to see the real you."

"That's a nice thing to say, but reality doesn't always work that way."

"You're right; it doesn't." He tugged her braided hair.

Her breath caught in her throat. It wasn't a strong pull, but damn if that didn't make her insides clench in delight.

Anthony smiled. "Hard limits?"

"It's probably quicker to tell you what I will do."

He raised his eyebrow.

She stiffened. "I told you: I'm new."

He laughed and tugged at her braid again. "You like me tugging on your hair, don't you?"

"For some reason, yes."

"Good. Go on. What will you do?"

"Light bondage and hands on my body."

He dipped his head closer to hers. "Spanking?"

"I don't know. It's a soft limit."

"Good. Since you're new to this, how about tonight I caress you, learn your body? Clothes on, unless you feel comfortable undressing."

Kaley's heart stopped for a second, then pounded in her chest. "I'm not ready to undress in public."

Anthony smiled. "This isn't really public, sweetheart, but I get it. How about we go to the massage table, and you let me show you?"

Could she do this? *Yes*, her body screamed. "Just touching?"

"Touching you all over and maybe an occasional swat to your ass. Is that acceptable?"

"Yes, Sir." Her words were breathless, airy, filled with nerves. But no fear. Kaley wasn't going to give herself time to back out of this. Wasn't this one of the reasons she'd come to Wicked Sanctuary? Plus, Noah had touched her, so this wasn't any different. She almost laughed out loud. Of course it was; Noah had been her instructor, Anthony was going to be a man she played with. Besides, Noah never made her blood heat the way Anthony did.

"Very good. Safe words?"

"Red to stop, yellow to slow down, and green to keep going."

"Excellent." He withdrew his hand from her neck, and Kaley instantly missed his touch, but he stood and helped her to her feet. Keeping hold of her hand, he led her across the club to the massage area. "Wait here." He let go of her hand and mounted the small stage.

She watched him clean the station, grab a blanket, and place it on the chair before coming back to her. He put his arm around her waist and guided her to the stage.

"Shall we start off with you on your stomach?"

"Yes, Sir." The words flowed from her without even thinking about it. Kaley climbed on the table. Anthony had left the pillow on the table, so she turned her head, bent her arms, and rested them above her head.

"I'm going to start off with your right arm and continue down your back to your legs and feet."

"Green, Sir."

"Close your eyes and concentrate on feeling my touch."

Kaley allowed her eyes to close, determined to let herself go with the flow and enjoy Anthony's touch.

Chapter 4

Anthony willed his dick to settle down. From the first *Sir* out of Kaley's mouth, it had jumped to attention and refused to back down. Until Kaley, his body's reaction had been rare. He only gave demos, which was the only time he played with a sub.

He didn't want to mess this up with Kaley. She was new and apprehensive about being in the club. He'd rein in his baser instincts if it killed him. With a light touch, he ran his fingers over her fingertips and down her arm. Gooseflesh popped out, and he grinned.

He kept his touch light as he continued down. He didn't mind that she was still dressed. This was about her getting comfortable with his touch and learning to trust him. Kaley was a novice, and the idea of teaching her excited him. Yes, he was attracted to her, and he still wanted to paint her, but it had become more than that.

She'd been so gentle with his grandmother when she found out about her injury, then there was Nugget. The Maltipoo wasn't known to make friends easily, yet Nugget jumped right into Kaley arms and greeted her like an old friend. That said something in Anthony's book.

After his third pass over Kaley's backside, he rested his palms on her ass. She inhaled sharply but didn't stiffen. Good. Slowly, he caressed her firm butt, his finger caressing the seam of her boy shorts.

She squirmed, and he lightly smacked her ass. "Please be still."

Her body flushed, but she instantly froze. A flash of pride went through him. He liked being a Dominant, and even with his knife play demos, it wasn't so much about the knives as it was messing with someone's head. It was a way for people to get out of their heads and really feel.

Hell, even some of the Doms he'd demonstrated on got lost in the sensations when they forgot he wasn't hurting them. Anthony liked playing with the knives, but he believed not only in Safe, Sane, and Consensual, but RACK. Risk Aware Consensual Kink.

Knife play wasn't for everyone, and he only did it when asked. Usually it was Max asking him to give a demo. But he wanted to see Kaley's creamy skin beneath one of his knives, to watch it blush and the fine hair rise with gooseflesh as he stroked her with the blade.

Anthony shook his head. Too soon. "Time to turn over." Standing next to the table, he braced it as he helped Kaley roll onto her back. Her skin was beautifully flushed and her breathing somewhat shallow.

"Are we doing okay?"

"Green, Sir."

"All right. I'm going to touch your breasts and pussy." She stiffened. "Over your clothing."

She bit her lower lip before softly saying, "Yes, Sir."

His dick pulsed. What was it about those words coming from her lips that caused his body to become so unruly.

Slowly, he traced the outline of her bra, keeping his touch light. Her nipples tightened and pressed against the fabric. Good. She was getting aroused. He avoided her nipples and moved over her abdomen.

When she sucked in a breath, he paused. "Keep breathing, sweetheart. You're beautiful."

Air whooshed out of her, and he continued his journey. Again, he traced the seam of the boy shorts. Heat met his touch. He kept his touch light and barely there. This was for her to get used to him. Not that he didn't want to dip his fingers beneath the fabric and see how wet she was, but that was for another time.

He moved away from her pussy and down her legs, caressing her legs and toes. Then he started back up her body. With each pass, she relaxed more and more. He picked up her arm, and it was languid in his hold.

"Kaley, sweetheart," he said softly.

"Yes, Sir." Her voice was barely there.

"I'm done."

Her lashes lifted. "Oh?"

"Easy." He placed his hand on her shoulder when she started to move. "Just lie there and relax for a few minutes, and tell me how you feel."

"Relaxed and confused."

"Confused about what?" She kept her eyes closed.

"You didn't play with my breasts or my…ummm…pussy."

Anthony grinned at the way she hesitated to say pussy, and it made him want her all the more. Except for the occasional demo, he hadn't scened or played in the community. He had in the past, just not at Wicked Sanctuary.

Was he getting jaded? He wasn't that old, only thirty, but he guessed Kaley was a few years younger.

"It's too soon for me to touch you there. We're just getting to know each other."

Her eyes opened, her gaze languid. "You're different." Her voice was soft.

"What do you mean?"

"I've talked with other Doms in the club; they wanted to go instantly into a full scene."

"In that sense, yes, I'm a little different. I want to get to know my sub before we start playing in the club. It's important to me."

"I like that." She flashed him a smile, then sat up.

Anthony grabbed the blanket and draped it over her shoulders. "Feeling okay?"

"Yes. That was wonderful. Thank you, Sir." She snuggled into the blanket.

"Excuse me." Anthony turned his head to see Rose.

"Hi, Rose."

"Sir." Rose inclined her head. "Kaley, Oliver and I will be ready to go home in about thirty minutes."

"Thanks, Rose. I'll meet you by your vehicle."

Rose nodded and walked away.

"That was good timing," Kaley said. She started to maneuver off the table, but Anthony was right there, taking her arm and helping her.

"Easy." He kept hold of her until he was sure she was steady on her feet. They might not have had a scene, but Kaley was totally relaxed.

"I'm good, Sir."

"Yes, you are."

Her cheeks turned pink, and Anthony was beguiled by her shyness. "I need to go put on some clothes."

"I'll walk with you."

"Okay."

Anthony accompanied Kaley to the bathroom, and when she went inside, he ducked into the men's room. Lucky for him, he didn't have to do much but slip on a jacket and grab his wallet, cell, and keys. Back in the hall, he leaned against the wall, waiting for Kaley.

Kaley had told Rose she would meet her by their vehicle. It sounded to him like Kaley was getting a ride with the couple. He wondered why. Kaley walked out in a pair of jeans and a simple blouse, her jacket over her arm and a small purse in her hand.

"You didn't have to wait for me."

"Yes, I did." He took her jacket and held it out for her. Kaley slipped one arm in, then switched her purse to her other hand and slipped the other arm in.

"Thank you."

"You're welcome." Cupping her elbow, Anthony led her through the reception area and out the front door to the parking lot.

"You don't have to come with me."

"I'm not going to leave you to wait out here by yourself."

"I'm a big girl."

"And I'm the big bad wolf; maybe I want a bite of you."

Kaley's laughter floated in the night air and caused Anthony to chuckle. "Is there something wrong with your van that you're getting a ride from Rose and Oliver?"

"The van is fine but too recognizable. I usually catch a ride in with Noah, and one of the subs gives me a ride home."

Anthony filed the information away. He would make sure he was the one to drive her home, and he'd talk with Noah about driving her to the club. He stopped where Oliver's SUV was parked and looked down at Kaley.

"I want to kiss you," he said softly.

"Please."

That was all the invitation he needed. Anthony cradled Kaley against his body and lowered his head. Her lips were soft and parted when he caressed them with his tongue. Kaley's arms wrapped around his neck and tightened.

Anthony couldn't help himself; he pulled her in tighter as he deepened the kiss. This woman could surprise him. This wasn't a shy kiss, but one from a woman who knew what she wanted. Her tongue played with his then retreated only to return a second later.

His cock stiffened against his zipper, and he shifted his stance. Kaley's fingers were in his hair, lightly stroking his scalp. In turn, he slipped his hand up her back, found her braid, and tugged it gently. She moaned into his mouth. Someone clearing their throat had him lifting his head.

"Hi, Oliver," Anthony said, still holding Kaley against him.

"Anthony. Do you need us to give you a few more minutes?" Oliver asked, amusement in his voice.

Anthony wanted to say yes, but now was not the time. "We're good." He looked down at Kaley. Her cheeks were flushed in the parking lot lighting. "I'll be in touch."

"Okay," she whispered.

Oliver unlocked the vehicle and helped Rose in. Anthony opened the rear passenger door for Kaley and helped her into the SUV. He brushed a quick kiss over her lips before he shut the door and backed away.

He stood there, watching as Oliver backed out, and waved as the vehicle pulled away. Tonight had been full of surprises. Now he had to process everything. He climbed into his own SUV and headed for home.

* * * *

"You and Anthony an item now?" Rose asked.

"I don't know what we are." Kaley stared out the window. Not that she could see much in the dark.

"But—"

"Behave, Rose," Oliver said.

"Yes, Sir," Rose responded, then fell silent.

Kaley ducked her head. Rose was curious, and Kaley didn't blame her, but how could she explain about her and Anthony when she didn't even know herself. Anthony wasn't as scary as she'd thought. They'd talked, and then he touched her, but not as much as she craved. And that was another thing to think through. How could she crave a man she'd just begun talking to?

Her skin still tingled from his caresses. He'd been so careful with his hands and fingers. By the time he was done, not only was she relaxed, but aroused. And he hadn't touched her sexually. He said he liked to go slow and learn her body. Well, that happened.

He'd been true to his word and hadn't mentioned her sitting for him to paint. But that kiss… She lifted her fingers to her lips. When he asked if he could kiss her, she hadn't even thought of saying no. She'd been more than ready for the kiss.

Anthony was all about consent, and she liked that about him. So many Doms wanted to jump right into the deep end, but he took his time, and with her being so new to the lifestyle, she appreciated it. Kaley bit back a laugh.

Maybe she was new to the lifestyle in practice, but she'd seen enough while growing up to know the difference between abuse and the lifestyle. She sighed. Tonight, Anthony made her feel desired, like she was worthy of his attention and care.

How long had it been since she felt that way? She couldn't remember. With both parents being alcoholics, she'd grown up taking care of herself and her siblings. At fourteen, she lied about her age to get a part-time job cleaning up at a vet clinic. She hid some of her money where her parents wouldn't find it and used the rest to buy food for her family.

Kaley closed her eyes. She'd moved on. It hadn't been easy. She'd stayed until the youngest was eighteen, then left and never looked back. Her brother and sister left as well, and they'd lost contact, so she wasn't sure where they were. They'd been determined to leave Pleasant Valley, but Kaley loved it here. She couldn't see leaving, especially since her parents were dead and even though her siblings were gone.

"Kaley," Oliver called her name.

"Sorry, I was lost in thought."

"You're home. I'll walk you in." Oliver hopped out of the vehicle.

"Thanks for the ride."

Rose turned to look back at Kaley. "I don't want to pry, but I need to say this. Anthony is one of the good ones."

"He is." She knew that instinctually.

Oliver helped her out of the SUV, waited as Rose locked the doors, then walked Kaley to her apartment. While she wasn't in the best neighborhood, it wasn't the worst either.

She waited while Oliver checked out her small one-bedroom apartment. "Thank you," she said when he stepped out.

"You're welcome." Oliver touched her arm. "If you need anything, you know to call Rose, right?"

Kaley smiled. "I'm good, Oliver, but yes, I know I can call if I need anything."

He nodded. "Get inside and lock up."

Kaley slipped inside her apartment and locked her door. Actually, she had more than one lock; there were also two deadbolts. She sighed. Would she ever get over the fear of a break-in? It was from her childhood. Her parents constantly forgot to lock the front door, and some mornings, she woke up to strangers in their house. Not that her parents cared. Kaley shrugged and padded to her bedroom.

Once there, she changed into her nightshirt and shorts before climbing into bed. At least tomorrow was Sunday, and she didn't have to get up early. She yawned. When she closed her eyes, all she could see was Anthony with his devil-may-care smile and twinkling eyes.

This was not good. Yes, she liked Anthony, but she really didn't have time for a man in her life. He'd sure helped her relax tonight. Anthony had allowed her to relax and be herself.

Turning over, Kaley stared into the semi-darkness, the night light from the bathroom chasing away the shadows. What was she going to do about him? It was obvious from his artwork that Anthony had money, and he probably came from money since she knew who his grandmother was.

And here she was, the girl from the wrong side of the tracks. Her education was high school and learning to be a groomer. No fancy degrees. She'd scrimped and saved for years, grooming for a pet store while working to get her van and start her own business.

She was successful. Fluff and Puff was four years old, and she was starting to turn a profit, which was nice, but she was also working six days a week, twelve hours a day. There was no time for dating or a relationship.

Kaley blew out a breath. A relationship? With Anthony? Wow, she'd taken one kiss to a whole new level. Anthony couldn't be interested in a relationship with her. She wasn't relationship material. He just wanted to have some fun with her at the club. That had to be it.

Could she handle that? Could she keep it simple, with no ties? She didn't have time for romance, but playing? Maybe. Closing her eyes, Kaley ran her hands down her body, imagining herself under Anthony's tender ministrations.

Oh, yeah. She could do that.

Chapter 5

"Anthony, darling boy."

His grandmother's voice jerked him awake. "Gran." He jackknifed off the sofa he'd been sleeping on.

"Easy, young man."

Anthony blinked to see his grandmother standing near him. "Sorry. What time is it?"

"Almost ten."

He shook his head to get rid of the cobwebs in his brain. "You should have woken me sooner." He hated that she'd waited for her breakfast. While she was getting around on crutches, she couldn't stand for long.

"I don't mind waiting, but I am getting hungry. I was able to feed Nugget."

"Okay. Give me five minutes, and I'll get breakfast going."

"Of course." His grandmother made her way out of the sunroom.

Anthony put his arms over his head and stretched, feeling the burn in his muscles after sleeping on the sofa— once he'd finished sketching in the wee hours of the morning. He quickly splashed water on his face and pulled on some clean clothes.

He hadn't been able to get Kaley out of his mind, so he sketched and sketched. Her. In each one, something was missing. Not that the sketches weren't good. They were. Something more was needed, and even though he'd been able to spend some time with her one-on-one, he still couldn't quite put his finger on it. Yet.

When he walked into the kitchen, he dropped a kiss on his grandmother's cheek. "What would you like today?" She'd been his lifesaver, and he was happy to do whatever he could for her.

His grandmother was the one who believed in him, who'd taken him in when his parents kicked him out because he wouldn't conform to their world.

"I'm in the mood for pancakes, if it's not too much trouble."

"Nothing you want is too much trouble." Anthony began pulling out everything he needed to make pancakes for her. He made quick work of well over a dozen pancakes before he sat down at the table.

They chatted as they ate. Anthony cleaned up the kitchen and dishes and yawned. "What's on the agenda for today?"

"I'm going to sit and binge-watch one of my shows. That breakfast will keep me full for a while." Anthony helped her rise to her feet, shuffle into the family room, and onto her favorite recliner. Once she was settled, he gave her the remotes and made sure she had her water glass and half-full pitcher next to her.

He yawned again. "Go." She waved her hand at him. "Take a nap, I'll be fine for a couple of hours."

"Yes, ma'am." Anthony made his way from his grandmother's house to his cottage on the property. He stripped in his bedroom and climbed into bed. A nap would be welcome. He set the alarm on his phone for two hours, then closed his eyes.

The vision of Kaley from last night played in his mind. She was so cute in her boy shorts and sports bra. But the way her eyes softened, how she sucked in a breath when he tugged her braid. His sub liked being restrained. At least that way.

His sub. He'd never really thought about having a sub before. Oh yes, he'd played with a couple of the subs in the club for demo purposes, but nothing more than that. He hadn't been in a relationship since high school.

It was by choice. Now that he was thirty, maybe it was time to start looking for a woman who would accept him for who he was. He groaned and rolled over. Old feelings he'd thought long-buried resurfaced. What woman would want him? The negative thought flowed through his consciousness.

Maybe it was time to see the therapist again. It'd had been a while since he had those negative thoughts. But he'd noticed recently they were creeping back. For now, he put it out of his mind. Sleep would help.

As he drifted off, the image of Kaley on the massage table, all relaxed with her rosy skin, stayed in his head, and his dreams were nothing short of erotic.

* * * *

Kaley rubbed her back as she climbed out of her van on Friday night. It had been a busy week. Anthony had never been far from her mind or her dreams. Night after night of sexy dreams had her reaching for her vibrator, and it couldn't take the edge off. And today, wrestling with a ninety-pound German Shepherd hadn't helped her back. For some reason, Apollo didn't want a bath this month. Kaley had to pick him up and put him in the tub—not easy. Then he chose not to stay. Thank goodness she'd closed the bathroom door, or she'd have had a much bigger mess to clean up.

She was wet and tired. Making sure the van was locked up, she trudged up the stairs to her apartment. Once inside, she locked the door and sighed. First things first, a shower. She went into the bathroom, stripped, turned on the water, gave it a few minutes to get warm, and stepped in.

A moan left her lips. The hot water felt good against her chilled skin, but she really couldn't stay in the shower long. She needed to do some bookkeeping tonight, look at tomorrow's appointments, and eat.

After drying off and dressing, Kaley stared at the contents of her fridge. She wasn't in the mood for cooking, so she grabbed the jelly, pulled out a loaf a bread and the peanut butter, and made a sandwich. One of the lessons she'd learned early on, peanut butter and jelly went a long way. She always made sure she had them on hand, along with bread.

Sandwich on a plate, she went to the small dining room table that doubled as a desk and opened her laptop. She found her financial ledger file and put in the day's earnings, then updated her spreadsheet and put in each client's date and amount.

Keeping good records was important. It made it so much easier to know which clients were regular and which were just occasional. Kaley munched on her sandwich as she input numbers, then pulled up her appointments.

Saturday was busy as normal. She had clients from eight until six. Not unusual. She checked the client's addresses against her map app and plotted out the best route. Then she sent an email to each client—along with a text—letting them know the approximate time she'd arrive.

With that done, she sat back in her chair and glanced at the clock. Eight-thirty, not bad. A little too early to go to bed, so maybe she'd start the romance book everyone was raving about. She pushed back from the table as her cell rang.

Unknown number. Not usual. It might be a client. "Fluff and Puff, this is Kaley."

"Hello, Kaley." Anthony's rich voice skimmed over her nerves.

Anthony? Kaley's heart skittered, and she worked hard to keep her voice steady as she answered. "Hi Anthony, what can I do for you?" He'd texted her, so why was he still an unknown number? Well, it might help if she put him in her contact list.

"I was hoping maybe tomorrow night we could have dinner together before going out to Wicked Sanctuary. That is, if I'm not being too bold."

Kaley laughed. She couldn't help it. "I thought all Doms were bold."

"We are. What do you say?"

Kaley thought for a moment. She really should say no. Dinner went beyond playing at the club. But she'd promised herself to always be honest with people, and he deserved to know her thoughts face to face not over the phone. "I won't finish with my last job until six-thirty."

"How about if I pick you up at seven-thirty? We can grab a bite and be at the club by nine. Oh wait, are you working the bar?"

"I have the ten to twelve shift tomorrow." It was nice he asked about her hours at the club.

"Great. What do you say?"

"Sure. Where are you taking me?"

"Nowhere fancy. You can wear normal street clothes."

"That works."

"Good. Now, I want you to think between tonight and tomorrow night about sitting for me."

"Anthony…" she started.

"Just think about it, please."

His please melted her resolve. "All right, I'll think about it, but I probably won't change my mind."

"Thank you." His voice was soft. "I've dreamed of you all week, my Kaley. See you tomorrow."

The line went dead, and she set her cell down with a sigh. Anthony was kind and considerate; any woman would date him. Kaley bit her lower lip. Anthony had been brought up so differently than she had. Better to let him know up front that she wasn't his type before he found out about her past. Shaking her head, Kaley reminded herself it was just dinner, not a proposal.

Trailer trash. The words made her stomach cramp. Until she got the job at the vet's office, how many times had she heard that in and out of school and as she did odd jobs around the neighborhood to pay for food for her and her siblings.

Kaley stood and stretched. Nope. She'd tell Anthony tomorrow night there could be nothing between them. He didn't need her kind of trouble or to hear the names that some people still called her. She put her plate in the sink, put her laptop away, and carried her cell into her bedroom.

The room was as plain as her life. White walls, a worn beige rug, a double bed with a brown comforter and tan sheets. Business was good, and it showed no sign of letting up. Soon, maybe she could have some nice things in her life. It really wasn't about material possessions, but she wanted to feel good about where she lived and her life, and saving everything she could was one of the steps.

A yawn escaped her lips. Bed time. She climbed into bed, and Anthony crept into her dreams once again. And in the dream, they were happy together.

Chapter 6

Kaley pulled her jeans on over her boy shorts and slipped on a blouse over her sports bra. Anthony would be here any minute. She'd run a few minutes over on her last job and barely had time to shower off. She threw her wallet and phone in her small purse, then grabbed her club bag, tossing her club shoes inside as the doorbell rang.

Rushing to the door, she dropped her purse on the side table, looked out the peephole, and threw the locks. "Hi, I'm running a few minutes late."

"Easy." Warm hands descended on her shoulders. "Breathe, sweetheart."

Kaley closed her eyes and took a deep breath. "Okay, I'm better. Thanks." She stepped back to let him in. Was that wise? Not that Anthony would hurt her, but her apartment was tiny and not very attractive.

"You have a nice place," he said, glancing around her apartment. The kitchen was right next to the front door, then the small dining area, and her living room. The bedroom door was slightly open, and the bathroom entrance was inside her bedroom. "But I don't like how easily someone can get into the building."

"There isn't much I can do about the front door lock. Most of us have complained, but our complaints fall on deaf ears." She'd given up, which was why she had so many deadbolts. "It's home."

"It's you. Subtle and uncluttered."

She wondered what he meant by that? How could it be her? She hadn't done much since moving in.

"Do you have everything in your bag?" He gestured to her hand.

"Yes, I just need to zip it and grab my purse."

"Let me." He took the bag from her, zipped it closed, and held onto it.

Kaley grabbed her purse, and soon, they were on their way. Anthony had a big black SUV. "What is it with guys and big SUVs?" she asked.

"Lots of room. Good to have during winter." He opened her door and helped her into the vehicle, then he put her club bag in the back seat before climbing behind the wheel. "Would you like to go to the Aztec Chef or Double D Barbecue?"

"Either one is fine with me."

"Let's do the barbecue." He pulled away from her apartment. "I'm guessing you had a busy day."

"Always. My last appointment of the day took longer than I anticipated. How was your day? How is Clara?"

"Gran is doing good. She's been using her crutches to get around and doing quite well."

"I'm glad. She's always been so active when I've groomed Nugget."

"It's hard for her to sit still right now, but she understands she needs to heal." He pulled into the parking lot and parked. Kaley reached for the door handle.

"Let me help you out." Anthony jumped out of the SUV, sprinted to her side, and opened the door.

"You know, I can do things on my own."

"Yes." He helped her out of the vehicle. "But I was raised to be a gentleman." The vehicle beeped as he locked it.

He held her arm as they walked into the restaurant. She wasn't used to men being this courteous. Well, most of the Doms in the club were, but outside of the club, there were a lot of assholes. Some of them were even clients.

"Good evening, table for two?" the hostess asked.

"Yes, please. I made a reservation under Anthony Payne, but we're a little late."

"Oh yes, Mr. Payne. You're fine; we have your table ready." The hostess led them to a booth. "Have a wonderful dinner."

Kaley slid in, and Anthony followed. She shifted when his thigh touched hers. He picked up the menus and handed one to her. She tried to ignore the way her skin tingled whenever they touched. Her awareness of Anthony was off the charts.

Opening the menu, Kaley began looking over her choices. So much food. Her stomach rumbled, reminding her she'd only had a PBJ for lunch.

"I heard that. Did you eat lunch?" Anthony asked.

Kaley lifted the menu so he wouldn't see her embarrassment. "I did but that was at least seven hours ago."

"I see." His voice deepened. "Lower the menu, please."

His voice was strong, and something inside her told her to obey. She closed the menu and set it down in front of her. Anthony's deep blue eyes watched her. "I don't like the idea that you may not be eating enough."

"It's fine." She shrugged off his concern.

"No, it's not." His forehead wrinkled. "You need to make sure you take time for lunch and a break where you can have a snack."

"I groom dogs and cats; there isn't always a lot of down time. Really, Anthony, I'm fine." Her darn stomach rumbled, calling her a liar.

"Good evening. I'm Mike, your waiter tonight. What would you like to drink?"

Kaley breathed out a sigh of relief at the waiter's interruption. "I'll have a diet soda, please."

"Beer, dark, if you have it."

"Indeed, we do, sir. I'll get your drinks and bring some bread." Mike walked away.

Anthony plucked her menu from where it sat in front of her. "Will you allow me to order for both of us?"

"I'd rather order for myself, thank you." She held her hand out for the menu. A little shiver went up her spine when he asked to order for her. Was he being a gentleman? Or was it some form of control? Kaley was beginning to feel like she was treading in very deep water.

"Very well." He handed her the menu. The waiter returned with their drinks and bread and asked for their order.

"I'll have the brisket dinner, beans, and a side salad with ranch dressing." Kaley shut her menu to see Anthony frowning.

"I'll have the beef platter with extra beans, mac and cheese, corn, and fries. And please bring us an extra order of rolls."

"I'll bring a variety of sauces as well," the waiter said then left.

"You must be hungry to order the beef platter," Kaley said. She'd read the descriptions. A full-rack of ribs, brisket, pulled pork, and tri-tip.

"I can always take home what I don't eat." There was something about the way he said the words that had Kaley wondering if he did this often. "Tell me more about Kaley."

She shifted her position. "Not much to tell."

"I doubt that. Did you grow up here in Pleasant Valley?"

"I did." She took a sip of her soda, gathering her courage. "I grew up in the Winter Village neighborhood." Kaley watched Anthony closely to see if he knew the place. She had to give him credit. He didn't flinch at the name.

Anthony nodded. "Not the easiest of neighborhoods to grow up in."

His tone was filled with compassion, not pity. Did he understand? "Yeah, I was glad when I got out."

"And when was that?"

"When I turned twenty. My siblings were both eighteen or over and could care for themselves." She took another drink of her soda.

"Parents?"

"There, but not." She swallowed. "They were alcoholics. They passed a few years ago."

Anthony had just picked up his beer and set it down abruptly.

"No, please. I don't mind if you drink a beer unless you plan on getting drunk."

"I don't drink to excess, a beer or glass of wine with dinner once in a while." He took a sip of his beer and turned toward her. "You tend bar at the club."

"Only because Max doesn't allow alcohol. Max understands that if a private party happens with alcohol, I won't bartend."

"Their alcoholism left a mark on you." He reached over and took her hand in his.

She couldn't deny his words. "It did. That's one of the reasons we can't work, Anthony." There. She said it.

"Oh?" His eyebrows rose. "Care to explain?"

Kaley swallowed. She wanted to say no, but for some reason, she felt she should explain. To give herself a minute to gather her courage, she grabbed a roll with her free hand and bit into it. "Oh my God, these are so good."

"Yeast rolls are the best." He kept his gaze on her. "Will you please answer my question?"

She finished off her roll. "I work really long hours."

"That's an excuse."

"Not really. I work six days a week, usually ten to twelve hours a day."

"I can accommodate your schedule." He squeezed the fingers he was still holding.

"That isn't fair to you."

"I didn't ask if it was fair. My schedule is a lot more flexible than yours."

The roll she'd eaten, as delicious as it was, sat like lead in her stomach. "I'm from the wrong side of the tracks." Her voice was soft.

Warm fingers cupped her chin and raised her face to his. "I don't care where you came from."

Her lips twitched. "You may not, but others will."

"The hell with them."

Kaley was startled by the venomous tone in his voice. "You say that now."

"I will always say it." He lowered his head. "You are your own woman. You got away from your family and made your own life, with your own business. Nothing else matters."

"You aren't real," she whispered. He couldn't be. Most men ran when they found out how she'd grown up.

"I'm very real." He sat back as the waiter arrived with their food. "Let's eat, then we can talk more."

She nodded and wondered how she was going to eat. But the smell of beef enveloped her, and her mouth watered.

* * * *

Anthony watched Kaley as she ate. He liked a woman with a healthy appetite but worried that Kaley's was because she hadn't eaten much during the day. That was something they'd have to work on. Did Kaley really think he was so shallow that her growing up in poverty would bother him? She would learn fast it didn't matter to him how or where she grew up.

She'd become a woman of strong mind and body. She owned Fluff and Puff and worked with animals. If he'd learned one thing when staying with his grandmother, it was that animals had a way of knowing the good guys and bad guys. There was a reason Nugget loved her and hated his parents.

Kaley pushed her plate away while it was still half full. "I can't eat another bite," she said when he looked at her.

He'd made a dent in the beef platter, but there was still a half-rack of ribs, half of the pulled pork, and most of the tri-tip, plus beans and corn. "If you'll excuse me for a moment, I need to go to the men's room."

Anthony slipped from the booth. He stopped their waiter and asked him to box up their dinner, but to put it in one bag. He'd leave it with Kaley. Something told him she didn't feel like cooking most nights, and the leftovers would be easy to reheat. He wanted to make her life a little easier.

After visiting the men's room, he made his way back to the table to see a man standing there. Kaley's face was red, and her eyes were shooting daggers at the man.

"Is this man bothering you, sweetheart?" he said as he came up to the table.

The man looked at him. Messy brown hair, and while he was well enough dressed for the restaurant, he reeked of alcohol.

"Just talking to an old friend," the man said.

"You were never a friend, Junior."

Anthony snickered, until the man spoke again, his voice rising.

"You were always trailer trash."

Anthony didn't hesitate. This wasn't something the entire restaurant needed to hear. He grabbed Junior by the shirt. "I think it's time to take out this trash." Anthony pulled Junior through the restaurant.

Applause broke out, telling him people had heard this man malign Kaley. His anger grew. He tossed her tormenter out the door. He stumbled but recovered.

"Better watch yourself; I have powerful friends," Junior yelled.

"So do I." Anthony waved his hand in dismissal and walked back inside. When he got to the booth, he sat down and noticed Kaley was trembling. "He's gone." Anthony slipped his arm around her shoulders.

"I'm sorry," she mumbled. "I should go."

"No." He tightened his arm around her. "None of this was your fault."

Her eyes widened, dark pools of misery and hope all in the same look. Who was this guy that Kaley was so emotional?

"I can't read minds, Kaley, but I won't let that prick ruin our night."

Their waiter came bustling up. "I'm so sorry about that. I was in the kitchen." He set the bag with their food on the table.

"Not your fault," Anthony said. It wasn't, but their waiter looked upset. "I would love some coffee and a dessert menu. Kaley?"

"I'm good."

The waiter rushed off.

Anthony didn't like how Kaley wouldn't look at him; instead, she was staring at the table. "Please look at me."

She shook her head.

He dropped his voice. "Kaley, honey. I want you to raise your eyes and look at me. Now."

She responded and lifted her head. Her gaze met his.

"That's better." He trailed his fingers over her hot cheek. "Who is Junior?"

"Someone I went to high school with." Her voice was soft.

Anthony shook his head. "There has to be more than that." The man was obnoxious.

"He was the captain of the football team and had his sights set on me because he thought I'd be easy pickings."

"Damn, I should have punched him."

"That's what he wanted." She closed her eyes and took a deep breath before she met his gaze again. "He learned quickly I wasn't interested."

"What did you do?" She was brave, even though there was a hint of fear in her eyes, and her voice was soft. She was so strong.

"Just introduced his family jewels to my knee."

Anthony winced. "And that makes him abuse you in a public place?"

She nodded. "I've seen him around town. He'll make snide comments, but I just ignore him. Trust me; I have clients who think I'm no better than the dirt on their shoes."

"Drop them." His anger returned. She didn't deserve to be abused by anyone.

"Someday, maybe. But, this is why we can't be together," she whispered.

"BS." He shifted the arm around her shoulders, and his hand clasped the back of her neck. Her intake of breath was swift, and her breathing changed. "Junior's an asshole, and you say some of your clients are too. You are not to believe a word they said."

"But it's true."

"Those words are never true." God, he hated that someone could cause her to retreat into herself. "You did what you did to survive. And you made it."

"I did survive." Her voice was a little stronger now.

"I'm sure others didn't, but you found your way, and now you're a successful business woman."

"I'm not sure I'd consider myself successful."

"Oh? How long have you been in the dog grooming business?"

"When I left home, I needed a job and a place to live. So I worked at a pet store and found a crappy little apartment." She shifted in her seat.

"The pet store allowed you to be around animals." He nodded at the waiter when he set down a cup of coffee and the dessert menu and left.

"Yes. The money was okay. I saved every penny I could, then I volunteered at the shelter when I wasn't working."

"Why the shelter?" She had such a big heart. "Why are you so drawn to animals?"

Her face lit up with a smile. "Animals have good instincts, but they also give unconditional love. I would feed strays when I was kid, even if it meant I didn't eat. The shelter gave me a chance to be with different types of dogs and cats. At the same time, I started taking online classes for grooming."

Another piece of the puzzle. She'd been doing this all on her own, working a job, volunteering at a shelter, and going to school. "That's a lot."

"Yeah, but it was heaven to me." She offered him a shy smile.

He nodded and picked up the dessert menu with his free hand. "Let's see. How does chocolate lava cake sound to you?"

"Delicious."

Anthony waved at the waiter and gave his dessert order. "How long before you actually groomed a dog?"

"Almost a year. It took me nine months to finish my online classes, then I did an apprenticeship with one of the groomers at the pet store."

"How long before you struck out on your own?"

"Four years. It isn't cheap to be a groomer."

"I imagine not." He'd seen the equipment she carted in to groom Nugget, plus the vehicle itself. Dessert arrived, and he picked up the fork, cut into the cake, and lifted a piece to her lips. His cock jumped as her lips closed over the fork.

He pulled the utensil back slowly and watched her chew and swallow with a dreamy look on her face.

"Absolutely yummy."

Anthony grinned and took a bite. "It is. How was it for you, striking out on your own, business-wise?"

"It was slow at first. I still worked part-time grooming at the pet store and once a week at the shelter. But business built. Your grandmother was one of my first clients."

"Nugget is her baby."

"It's so nice of you to stay with her while she's healing."

His lips twitched. "Actually, I live on the property, so it's no hardship for me to sleep on the sofa in the sunroom for a few weeks." It wasn't. He owed his grandmother more than he could ever repay.

"That's nice. To be close to family." There was a wistful note in her voice.

He fed her another piece of cake while he thought about her words and dismissed them. It was nice to be close to his grandmother, but not his parents. Or should he say—adoptive parents. He glanced at his watch. It was almost eight thirty, and he needed to get Kaley to the club for her bartending shift.

"I hate to end this, but we need to get to the club."

"Oh goodness, I totally forgot." She pulled away from him, and he let her go.

Anthony drank his coffee and motioned the waiter over. "Bill, please."

"No bill, sir. The manager took care of it as a thank you for you removing the patron who was causing a fuss." The waiter walked away.

Anthony stood and held his hand out to Kaley to help her up.

"That was nice of them," she said.

"But not necessary." Anthony grabbed the bag with their leftovers, and they walked to his SUV.

* * * *

Kaley slipped behind the bar right before ten. Noah handed a soda to a club member and raised his eyebrows. Dang, the place was hopping tonight. She nodded at Noah and began getting drinks. After twenty minutes, the crowd thinned out.

"I was beginning to wonder if you were going to show up," Noah said. "You're usually here long before your shift starts."

"Sorry. Anthony took me to dinner, and we lost track of time." That was a first for her. Even with the uncomfortable conversation, she was at ease mentioning Anthony.

"No worries." Noah kissed her cheek. "Can you cover until one? I want to scene tonight."

"Sure. Have fun."

Noah gave her a wicked look before he stepped out from behind the bar.

Kaley began serving drinks, and Anthony took a seat at the end of the bar. He was staring at her. She worked her way toward him. "Do you want a drink?"

"I'm good. Was Noah upset?"

"No, just making sure I'd cover until one. Noah wants to scene tonight."

"I see. I'm not sure I like him kissing you, even if it's on the cheek."

"He's a friend, nothing more." Kaley kept her gaze on Anthony; he didn't look jealous, and he had no reason to be.

"All right." More people filled the bar. "Come and talk to me when you can."

Kaley nodded and moved away. They'd dropped their conversation over dinner because of the time, but she knew Anthony wouldn't forget.

How could she make him understand that them together was not a good idea. He had money; she didn't. Even Junior showing up tonight shook her up. *Trailer trash.* She hated those words with a passion. Would she ever stop thinking of herself like that? She wasn't trash to be thrown away, and she'd never lived in a trailer in her life. While there were some very beautiful trailers out there, her family home hadn't been much better than one of those trashy trailers on cinderblocks. She sighed. Maybe she could convince Anthony on the drive home.

* * * *

It was after two before they got out of the club, and Kaley couldn't stop yawning. Anthony didn't say much as he drove her home. When he parked in front of her apartment building, she waited. He had told her he preferred to help her in and out of the vehicle.

"Thank you for dinner."

"I'm coming in and making sure your apartment is safe."

She opened her mouth, but the look in his eyes told her he'd argue with her all night, and she'd still do what he wanted. With a nod, she started for the front door. Anthony reached around her and pushed the lobby door open as she reached it.

They walked down the hall. "I'd feel better if you were on one of the upper floors."

Kaley shivered. "Trust me; the first floor is the best." He waited until she unlocked the door, then he went inside and held his hand up for her to wait. She propped her hip against the door frame and waited. All she wanted to do was change and get into bed.

"All clear. Lock the doors after me, and if you feel unsafe, call me."

"Yes, Sir."

"You better believe it. We'll continue our conversation later this week." He leaned down and brushed a soft kiss against her lips, then pulled the door closed behind him.

Kaley flipped all the locks and turned. That's when she saw the white plastic bag sitting in her kitchen. Anthony must have brought her leftover dinner in. She remembered him saying he stuck it in the fridge at the club.

Grabbing the bag, she pushed it into her fridge with a frown. That seemed like an awful lot of food for what she had leftover. She'd deal with it tomorrow. Shutting the fridge, she made her way into her bathroom. A quick brush of the teeth, a change of clothes, and she was climbing into bed. Tomorrow would be filled with office work, verifying next week's appointments, and making sure all her equipment was clean and in working order.

Chapter 7

The following weekend, Kaley rushed into Wicked Sanctuary and into the ladies room. Damn! She was running late again, and she hated that. Her last appointment of the day was a client she wasn't fond of, and tonight, he got a little handsy.

She didn't want to fire a client, but she recognized there was no other recourse here. Inappropriate remarks and inappropriate contact were non-negotiable. Kaley confronted him and told him if he didn't stop harassing her not only would she tell his wife, she'd file a sexual harassment suit against him, and a restraining order as well.

He'd backed away so fast she thought he was going to run. In the van, her hands were shaking after the confrontation, but she was proud of herself for standing up to him. She'd called Anthony and told him she'd grab a ride with one of the subs. Luckily for her, Oliver and Rose hadn't left for the club yet.

Once behind the bar, Kaley noticed the music was heavier; there must be a lot of flogging tonight. The Doms loved music with an intense beat. She glanced around. It looked like a normal Saturday night. She settled in for her shift. At least it wasn't a late one. Noah would take over at ten, and then Ward at one.

When ten rolled around, Kaley looked for Anthony. He'd stopped at the bar when he came in and then told her he was going to help another Dom for a bit. She noticed he was at the bondage station.

She made her way into the sub area and tucked her legs under her as she sat down. The week from hell was catching up with her. She'd been up at five every morning, not getting to bed until ten or later, and after dealing with her client today, it had all been too much.

Settling her arm on the back of the sofa, she laid her head on her arm. She could still see Anthony on the stage, talking with the Dom. She smiled. Anthony looked so delicious in the muted light, and she loved watching his muscles in his arm and back playing over his tight t-shirt.

Her eyes were so heavy. She'd rest for a few minutes while she waited for him.

* * * *

Anthony left the stage and glanced at the bar. Noah was there, so where was Kaley? He looked over at the sub area. There she was. He walked over and realized she was sound asleep.

They'd talked during the week. She'd been working over twelve-hour days. He was worried she wasn't getting enough sleep. How could anyone sleep with all the noise in the club? She must be exhausted.

He saw a Dom approach her. Nope, not happening. Anthony started toward the Dom, but he shrugged and walked away. Anthony stopped and looked around for Max. He saw him standing by the bondage chair.

"Max," he said quietly.

"Hey, Anthony. What do you need?"

"Is there a private room available?" At least Kaley could rest in a quieter place.

Max frowned. "I'm not sure Kaley is ready for that."

"She's not." He gestured to the sub area. "She fell asleep, and I just want someplace where she can have some quiet until I can take her home."

"I see. Meet me at room four."

Anthony crossed to the sub area and picked Kaley up in his arms. She murmured something and laid her head on his shoulder. With careful steps, he carried her along the outskirts of the play area until he came to the private rooms.

"I can't lock the door," Max said, opening it.

"No worries, I'll be sitting at her side in case someone comes in."

Max nodded, and Anthony strode into the room. The door closed behind Max, the click loud in the quiet room. Max must have soundproofed these additions to Wicked Sanctuary. The lighting was subtle, and he grinned. This room was themed as the spanking room. He laid Kaley on the black sheets before finding a blanket in the cabinet to cover her.

He pulled the black leather chair over and sat down. The room had potential when Kaley was ready. There was a spanking bench, a St. Andrew's Cross. Next to the cabinet with the blankets was an array of implements, all for impact play.

Relaxing against the leather, Anthony wished he had his sketch book with him. He had one in his vehicle, but didn't want to leave Kaley alone. But maybe… He stood and opened the door. Luckily, Dane was walking by.

"Hey, Dane."

"Anthony. Do you need something?" Dane looked over his shoulder.

"A favor. Can you watch Kaley while I run out to my SUV and grab something?"

"Sure. I'll stand out here and make sure no one bothers her."

"Thanks." Anthony closed the door and maneuvered past the crowd. Once he retrieved his keys, he sprinted to his vehicle and returned to the private room in no time.

Dane nodded and walked away as Anthony opened the door. Kaley was curled up on her side, still asleep. Anthony took his seat, rested his left ankle on his right knee, and opened his sketch pad.

His fingers flew over the paper, page after page. He was amazed how sketching Kaley in person brought her to life on the page, even as she slept. He also realized that his desire to capture her with oils on canvas had changed from infatuation to need.

After a while, Anthony stopped, set his sketch pad and pencils on the side table, stood, and stretched. He had no idea what time it was. It didn't matter. Max knew they were in here. After walking around the room for a few minutes, he sat again and leaned his head back.

"Anthony."

Anthony jerked awake to see Max standing next to him.

"Sorry, I must have dozed off." He glanced at the bed. Kaley was still out. She must've been exhausted to sleep through all of this. Yes, it was time they talked about the hours she worked.

"No worries. It's almost three, and we're going to close at four."

"All right. If Kaley isn't awake by the time you're ready to close, I'll wake her."

Max nodded and left the room. Anthony yawned and stood. His back popped as he stretched. That would teach him to sleep in a chair, even one as comfortable as the leather one. Kaley stirred, and Anthony turned toward the bed.

There was confusion in her eyes as she sat up abruptly. "Easy, Kaley." He kept his voice soft.

"Anthony?" She ran her hand over her face. "Where am I?"

"One of the private rooms." He strode over to her. "You fell asleep in the sub area. I carried you in here so you could rest."

"Oh my goodness." Her cheeks turned red. "I only meant to close my eyes for a minute."

"That's all it takes."

She swung her legs over the side of the bed, and Anthony sat next to her. "We need to talk about your workload."

"Not tonight." She covered her mouth as she yawned. "What time is it?"

"A little after three."

"Three in the morning?" Her eyes widened.

"Yep. Come on, let's get changed." He stood and picked up his sketch pad and pencils, before taking her hand to help her up. The perfect excuse to touch her.

Kaley glanced around the room as he pulled her up, and her breathing grew shallow. "I've never been in a private room before."

He grabbed the blanket off the bed. "You're too new to the lifestyle." Anthony leaned down. "But one day, we'll play in this one."

"I'd like that, Sir," she whispered.

His dick jumped with her words. Kaley was adventurous, and he liked that. He dropped the blanket in the hamper by the door and guided her out. The club was almost empty, and Max stood by the bar.

Anthony waved at him, and he nodded.

"Should I go say something?" she asked.

"Like what?" Anthony was curious what she would say to Max.

"I don't know. Something like, sorry I fell asleep, thank you for letting us use the room." Her cheeks flushed again. "That sounds stupid."

"No, it doesn't." He led her to the ladies room. "Max understood. Go get changed, and I'll meet you back here."

Kaley nodded and disappeared into the bathroom. It took Anthony only a few minutes to pull on a shirt and get his stuff. Max waited in the hall.

"Kaley okay?" Max asked.

"Yeah. A little embarrassed she fell asleep."

"I have to say that's a first." Max chuckled.

Kaley walked out of the ladies room with Sierra. "Don't stress over it, Kaley," Sierra was saying.

Anthony frowned. "What are you stressing over, sweetheart?"

Her cheeks grew red. "It's nothing."

Sierra shook her head, and Anthony took the hint. "Let's go." He cupped her elbow.

"Thank you, Master Max,"

"You're welcome," Max said before glancing at Anthony. Max dropped a kiss on Kaley's forehead. "Get some rest."

"Yes, Master Max."

"Thanks, Max," Anthony said, then led Kaley out of the club and over to his SUV. The parking lot was almost empty. He opened the passenger door and helped her in.

She'd already fastened her seatbelt when he climbed behind the wheel. He started the engine. "It will take a few minutes to warm up." He noticed her shivering.

"I'm fine."

He didn't argue with her, but they'd talk about her saying she was fine when it was obvious she wasn't.

"I'm sorry," she said softy as he drove back to town.

"About what?" He glanced at her. She was twisting her fingers together.

"Falling asleep on you. And keeping you up so late."

"You don't need to apologize." He took one hand off the wheel and captured her hand in his. "But I would like to discuss your work schedule."

Her sigh was loud, and she clamped a hand over her mouth.

Anthony chuckled. "I'm hoping that wasn't an annoyed sigh."

"No."

He glanced at her.

"Okay, maybe."

"I couldn't miss how exhausted you are." He squeezed her hand.

"I'm usually not like that. This was just a super busy week and..."

"And, what?"

"It's a work thing and I have it under control."

All of his protective instincts came to life. "Tell me." His fingers tightened around the steering wheel.

"I had to fire a client today. He was being a total ass, making comments that were thinly disguised sexual harassment, and he kept invading my personal space. Non-negotiable. I fired him on the spot."

Anthony ground his teeth together to stop himself from demanding the man's name so he could go teach him some manners. "I want to punch the guy."

"After the way you handled Junior, that's why I wasn't going to say anything." Her fingers tightened around his. "But since we've started seeing each other—even if casually—I wanted to be honest."

His anger drained away. She was protecting him. "Thank you for telling me." He lifted her hand to his lips and kissed the back of it. Time to change the subject. "Why didn't you beg off the club?" They'd talked about Saturday night at the club all week. "I wouldn't have minded."

"I wanted to honor my commitment to Max." She shifted in her seat.

"Max would have understood."

"It wouldn't have been fair to the others." She blew out a breath. "Noah and the others who help with the bar depend on me. I don't take that responsibility lightly."

"I can understand that, but you need to take care of yourself as well." She probably wasn't aware of how much he watched her. She had a generous heart, and that made her vulnerable.

"I know." Another sigh escaped her lips. "I'll do better."

He squeezed her hand and didn't comment. Their budding relationship was too new for him to go overboard. When he parked outside her apartment, a group of teenagers was out front on the sidewalk in front of her building. Pretty unusual for after three in the morning. After helping Kaley from the vehicle, he gripped her arm.

"Hey, Frankie. Aren't you out late?" Kaley said as they walked to the front door.

"I'm fine, Miss Kaley. Just talking," the young man replied.

"All right, but don't worry your families."

"Yes, Miss Kaley," the group answered.

Anthony held his questions until he'd checked her apartment out. "Those boys out there?"

"They live in the neighborhood. They're not bad kids, just a little lost." She yawned.

"Lock up and get some rest. We'll talk tomorrow." Anthony kissed her, keeping it light. He pulled the door closed behind him and waited until he heard the locks click. Then he walked back outside. There were still three teenagers out there, including the one Kaley called Frankie.

"Are you Miss Kaley's boyfriend?" Frankie asked.

"Working on it." His gaze took in the boys. They were clean, and their clothes were typical of teenagers.

"Good. She needs to get out of this neighborhood," Frankie said. "It isn't the best place."

Anthony didn't like the sound of that. "Problems?"

"Not yet, but you never know, and Miss Kaley is a good person. I try to keep an eye on her. She doesn't have much, but she's always feeding us."

Another piece of the Kaley puzzle. Anthony pulled out his cell phone. "You got a cell?"

"Yeah."

Anthony gave Frankie his number. "If you ever need anything or you notice Kaley needing help, call me. I don't care what time of the day or night."

"Thanks, man." The three teens wandered off down the street.

Anthony climbed into his SUV. He wanted Kaley to be safe. He couldn't make her move, but that didn't mean he couldn't do some upgrades for her. Maybe he and a couple of the guys from the club could have a chat with her landlord about the front door.

Plan forming, Anthony drove home. Tomorrow, or should he say today, was Sunday, and he was looking forward to it.

Chapter 8

Kaley woke by nine on Sunday. She wasn't surprised. She'd slept in the club for well over five hours, and once home, she fell into bed and slept another five hours. After eating some cereal, she went to work on her finances. The paperwork for her business was never-ending.

Things were looking good. She sent out confirmations for all her appointments and checked all her equipment. It was just noon. She was at loose ends for the first time in a while. Without thought, she called Anthony. Maybe they could get coffee and talk.

"Well, hello, Kaley. To what do I owe the honor?"

His husky voice sent shivers of awareness through her.

"If you aren't busy, how about we get a cup of coffee and chat."

"I'd love that, but I have a standing appointment at one."

"Oh." She tried to keep the disappointment out of her voice.

"Why don't you come with me, and we can have that coffee and chat afterward. I'll be done by three."

"Won't I be in the way?"

"Nope. What do you say?"

Kaley was intrigued. "I'd like that."

"Great." The excitement in his voice made her smile. "I'll pick you up in thirty minutes. Dress casual."

The line went dead, and Kaley stared at her cell. Casual was about all she had.

* * * *

"Where are we going?" Kaley asked as Anthony drove away from her apartment.

"It's a surprise." He executed several turns and then pulled into the parking lot of the rec center.

"What's here?" He helped her from the vehicle.

"My standing appointment." Anthony took her hand and began walking.

Kaley saw there were a lot of cars in the lot, but again, it was a recreation center; they were probably playing basketball on a Sunday. She glanced at Anthony. If he was going to be playing, he wasn't exactly dressed for it.

"Hi, Gladys," he said, waving at the white-haired woman behind the counter.

"Anthony, everyone is waiting."

"Great." Anthony walked down the hallway and into a room. Kaley's mouth dropped open. There had to be twenty kids waiting for him, and there were easels with canvasses all over the room, as well as art papers on a long table in front of the easels.

"Mr. Anthony," yelled a boy Kaley guessed to be about ten.

The next thing she knew, she and Anthony were swarmed by the kids. Kaley couldn't stop smiling. They were of varying ages, all talking at the same time. She felt a tug on her arm and glanced down to see a young girl with crazy blonde curls and an impish smile.

"Are you Mr. Anthony's girlfriend?" Her voice was full of awe.

How did she answer that?

"Jazzy, this is my friend, Kaley." Anthony clapped his hands. "Okay, everyone settle down and take your seats." The kids moved to the tables or easels. "Let's start with something easy today. I want you to draw a sunset at the ocean."

Heads bent, the kids went to work. "You're teaching them art?"

"Yes." He guided her over to a chair. "Want your own easel?"

Kaley shook her head. Every time she'd tried freeform art, she'd failed. This was not her forte.

"Have a seat while I work."

Kaley watched as Anthony made his way around the room. He stopped to talk to each student, giving hints and showing them techniques. When he arrived at the easels, he spent more time talking about blending colors.

She realized the students at the easels were more advanced than the ones at the table. But Anthony didn't linger long. He made sure he divided his attention among all the kids. This was a different side of him. All she'd ever seen on TV or movies, and read portrayed most artists as moody and uncommunicative.

But not Anthony. He seemed in his element here. He stripped off his shirt to prevent paint from getting on it revealing a sleeveless t-shirt, and when he went to help one of the kids, she saw the tattoo on his upper arm. A pile of books with an artist's palette on top. That made sense, since he was an artist. When he turned, she saw the tat on his other arm. A knife through a rose.

She wondered about that. Beautiful but deadly were the first words that came to mind. Her fingers itched to trace his ink. The designs revealed a lot about the man who was a mystery to her. When he walked over and handed her his shirt, he leaned down. "The kids are asking all sorts of questions about you."

"Oh?" Why were they interested in her? "I'm not that interesting."

"To them you are. I've never brought a woman with me to class."

Kaley blinked, and Anthony moved away. She almost called him back but decided to stay quiet and just watch. There were so many facets to him, and she wanted to explore each one. At two-thirty, Anthony told the kids to finish and start cleaning up.

He strode up to her. "I hope you weren't bored." He took his shirt from her and put it on. Part of her was sorry he was covering up his art work. In that moment, she realized that, whenever she saw him, the shirts he wore covered his ink.

"You keep your tats covered. Why?"

"Habit." He shrugged.

Kaley stood and walked over to the table to help some of the kids put their art materials away. She was impressed. Each child had a box with their name on it. They put all their materials in the box, and closed the lid. Each box was then put on a shelf at the back of the room.

Anthony helped those with paints, instructing them on proper cleaning of their brushes and storage. He was gentle with each kid, but it was more than that. He showed patience and kindness, never making anyone feel bad about anything they did.

"Roll up your work so you can take it home and show your parents. Painters, be careful as you carry your canvas out. The paint will still be damp, so lay it flat with the picture up so it can continue to dry."

Footsteps sounded, and Kaley turned to see a group of adults, obviously the children's parents, walk into the room. They smiled, and several thanked Anthony for teaching the class. In less than twenty minutes, all the parents and kids had left.

"I'm impressed," Kaley said as they drove away from the center.

"It's not a big deal. It gives the kids something fun to do while giving the parents a bit of break." He turned left. "Do you mind if we have coffee at Gran's house? I don't like leaving her too long. She'll get impatient and try to do things on her own."

"I don't mind at all."

"Thank you." He flashed her a grin.

The drive didn't take long. "Gran, I'm back," Anthony called as he walked in. "I've got Kaley with me."

"Wonderful," Clara called. "I'm in the kitchen."

They walked into the kitchen and found Clara seated with her foot elevated on a small stool. Nugget saw Kaley, jumped off Clara's lap, and ran over to Kaley, jumping up for attention.

"Hello, Clara." Kaley knelt down and cuddled Nugget. "And to you, Nugget."

"I'll start the coffee," Anthony said.

"Would you help me to my room first? I'd like to lie down for a while." There was a twinkle in Clara's eyes.

Anthony was at Clara's side in an instant. "Are you feeling okay?" Kaley could see the bond between grandson and grandmother. She sighed silently. She'd never known her grandparents. Didn't even know if they were still alive.

"I'm fine, dear. Just want a little nap." Clara glanced at Kaley. "It's good to see you with Anthony."

Kaley's cheeks heated.

"Gran." Anthony groaned.

"All right." Clara waved a hand. "I'll behave. Come on, Nugget."

Kaley shook her head as the pair left the room. She crossed the room and began making coffee.

"You didn't have to do that," he said when he got back.

"It's fine. Is Clara okay?"

"She's fine. I think she wanted to give us some alone time."

Kaley glanced at the floor.

"Sit down. Gran told me where she keeps the good cookies."

Kaley laughed. "Good cookies?"

"That means fresh baked chocolate chip cookies." He opened the cabinet and pulled out a container. When he opened the lid, the smell of chocolate wafted through the kitchen, and her stomach growled. "Someone is hungry."

The coffee pot gave its last gurgle as Anthony put the cookies on a platter. He poured two cups of coffee. After carrying them to the table, he grabbed the platter of cookies and the milk out of the fridge.

"Sorry, no cream just milk." How did he know she liked cream with her coffee? He must have seen her with coffee at the club. The man was too observant. He set the items on the table before taking his seat.

"It's fine." Kaley poured some milk in her coffee and then grabbed a cookie. She ate it in two bites. It was so soft and delicious. "These are fantastic."

"Gran likes to bake. I did oven duty yesterday. If I hadn't, she would have done it herself."

"How much longer before she can get around on her own?"

"We see the doctor next week."

Kaley nodded. "How long have you worked with the kids?"

"For a year now. Most of them are underprivileged kids or with bad home situations or from a single parent family. This gets the kids out of the house and in a place where they can express themselves."

"Has it been the same kids for the year?"

"Most of them. Some disappear, and it takes some detective work to find out they've moved, or they simply have parents who won't allow them to go anymore."

"That's sad."

"It is, but I do what I can."

"I think you do a lot." Kaley had to wonder if, when she was growing up, she'd had something like that, would things have been different.

"Have you given any more thought to sitting for me?" Kaley's eyes widened.

"Thought I forgot about that, didn't you?" He grinned.

"I don't know. I'm not model material."

"You said that before. You're model material for me."

She shook her head and looked down at the platter of cookies. Goodness, over half of them were gone. Had she really eaten that many?

"Look at me, please."

His voice was soft and compelling. Kaley lifted her head to find kindness and confusion in his eyes.

"Please explain to me why you believe modeling for me would be such a bad thing."

Kaley almost snorted. "You have eyes."

"I do." He stood and held out his hand. "Come with me, please."

She didn't hesitate and placed her hand in his. He guided her from the kitchen to the sunroom. He was still using it as a studio. There were several drop cloths on the floor, and canvases in various states littered the room.

Anthony led her over to a full-length mirror leaning against the wall. He stopped and pulled her in front of him, his arms loosely around her waist. She squirmed.

"Be still." The words were spoken firmly yet softly in her ear.

She instantly complied.

"Better. Now, eyes on us in the mirror."

Kaley didn't want to look, but his voice was compelling. She raised her gaze until it met his in the mirror.

"I don't know what you see, but I see a beautiful woman. She has kind brown eyes and deep red hair that makes me think of sunset on a winter's evening."

She opened her mouth, but his fingers touched her lips, stopping her words.

"Soft lips that taste like sweet candy. A body that could stop traffic if not hidden beneath clothes that do nothing for her shape." His arm tightened around her waist when she would have squirmed free.

How could he say these things about her? She had eyes. She was nothing like he was describing.

"Her breasts are firm." His hands slid from her waist to cup her breasts.

Her breath caught in her throat. This felt different from when he touched her in the club. More sensual.

"They fit so perfectly in my hands." He squeezed both, and she shifted from one foot to the other. His hands skimmed over her stomach, past her waist, to the top of her thighs.

"Anthony," she whispered.

"Spread your legs for me, sweetheart."

Kaley did as he asked. His palms slid to the inside of her thighs, then his right hand cupped her pussy. The sound she made in her throat amplified the heat low in her belly.

"Soon, I'll touch you there, and my fingers will make you hot and wet." His fingers traced the seam of her jeans, and Kaley couldn't catch her breath. "Then I'll spread you wide and feast on your sweetness until you're shaking beneath me."

She was already shaking. His words set off mini earthquakes inside her tummy in anticipation of his actions.

"When I decide you're suitability aroused, then and only then will I sink my cock into your warm wetness."

Kaley pressed her ass against him. His hardness pressed into her butt with delicious pressure. She was aroused. More than that, she wanted Anthony to do what he was describing.

"Soon," he whispered and kissed her temple before moving his hands back to her waist.

She almost cried out for him to continue, but his next words took her voice away.

"You are more than beautiful on the outside; you're beautiful on the inside."

He couldn't mean that. She opened her mouth, but he didn't give her a chance to say anything.

"You are patient with the animals you groom and with people. You have patience most people would envy. You are sure of yourself and very competent." His arms tightened around her waist.

"Thank you," she whispered, needing to say something. Her body still yearned for his, but it would remain unfilled for now.

"You have a great compacity for love, but it's been stifled."

That hit too close to home for Kaley.

"One day, you'll trust me to tell me the whole story, but for today, I want you to see what I see. This is the woman I want to paint. The woman who is kind, generous, and has a beauty that radiates from the inside out."

"I'm not all that." She glanced at her feet.

"You are." His lips brushed her cheek. "This is what I see. Will you let me paint what I see?"

"I still don't know."

"Maybe some of this will change your mind." He spun her away from the mirror and began taking cloths off paintings on easels. Finished paintings.

"Oh my." Her breath caught in her throat. The first painting was of a spanking scene, although she couldn't see anything private. The woman was bent over the spanking horse, her butt painted in various shades of red. There was a large male hand resting on the curve of her ass, as if caressing it.

"He's rubbing the sting from her skin and letting her know he's there for her."

Kaley could almost feel the man's touch. Anthony had captured the moment perfectly.

"Then there's this one." He whipped off another cloth.

This one was his grandmother holding Nugget. "That's beautiful."

"Since Gran has been laid up, she finally allowed me to paint her." He moved to the next canvas.

Kaley's heart stuttered her in chest at the sensuality of the next painting. Two men in an embrace, both bare chested, but it was the way each held the other. The trust and love shining from their eyes captured her attention.

"Anthony, you are a fantastic artist. It's no wonder Dane is showcasing you in his gallery."

"I got lucky."

She turned to him and put her hand on his arm. "Not luck. You are amazing. Until Dani took me into the gallery, I hadn't realized how talented you are."

"When did Dani take you to the gallery?"

"Right after we met. The day I came to groom Nugget."

"You're not offended?"

"What?" Her eyes grew wide. "This is beautiful art. It shows life. I don't know how to explain it, but when I look at the picture of the two men embracing, I see the love they have for each other."

"Some see my art and call it dirty."

He watched her intently. Was he waiting for her to show contempt? No, she never would. Anthony's art showed beauty and love and all things good. Anyone who didn't see that was blind.

"They are small, jealous people." She stepped closer and hugged him. His arms closed around her, and Kaley found herself cocooned in warmth.

"I'm asking again, will you allow me to paint you?"

Kaley tilted her head back and stared up at him. "I'm still not sure." She glanced at the pictures he'd uncovered and then back at him. "I need to be totally comfortable with it before I make a decision."

"I understand. But that doesn't mean I'll stop asking."

"Pushy Dom."

"Naturally." He brushed his lips over hers. A chime sounded, and Anthony sighed. "That's my reminder to get dinner started. You're staying for dinner."

"You're telling me. Not asking?"

"Right. I'm feeding you dinner. Come along so you can sit and watch."

Kaley gave the paintings one last look as Anthony pulled her from the room.

* * * *

Dinner was a lively affair. Anthony made spaghetti with meatballs and garlic bread. Kaley sat at the kitchen table, watching him work. They chatted about all sorts of things, and Kaley realized they had a lot in common.

When Clara came into the kitchen, Anthony rushed to help her. He was a good man. Nugget laid at Kaley's feet as she chatted with Clara. By the time dinner was ready, Kaley's mouth was watering.

"I know you don't drink," Anthony said, staring into the contents of the refrigerator.

"Water is fine."

"Not with my food," he said.

Kaley shook her head. He was trying so hard to find her something to drink.

"I've got it." He started pulling ingredients from the fridge and then pulled out a blender.

"Don't go to so much trouble."

"It's no trouble. The sauce has another ten minutes." He began chopping up something and putting it into the blender. In a few minutes, he was filling some tall glasses with a peach-colored drink.

"Non-alcoholic Peach Bellini for my favorite ladies." He presented his masterpiece to Clara and Kaley.

Kaley picked up the drink and took a sip. The peach flavors exploded against her taste buds. "This is so good."

"Wait until you try his meatballs," Clara said.

"Are there Italians in your family?" With a last name like Payne she didn't think so, but then what did she know?

"Not a lick that I know of." Anthony busied himself at the stove.

"He likes to cook and taught himself," Clara said.

Kaley smiled. "I'm glad he does and did."

Anthony set a big bowl of pasta on the table, the sauce in another bowl, then a platter of meatballs. "And I can't forget." The last platter was garlic bread. He glanced at Kaley who subtly pointed to his grandmother.

He grinned. "Gran, how much do you want?"

"Fill my plate. Whatever I don't finish I can have tomorrow."

Anthony turned his head and winked at Kaley, then filled his Gran's plate from the bowl of pasta, before handing it to Kaley.

Chapter 9

"I can't eat another bite," Kaley said, pushing back from the table. "Anthony, you are a wonder in the kitchen as well."

"I have lots of talents." He winked.

"Nothing this old lady needs to hear. I'm going to go watch TV." Clara waved Anthony away when he started to help her. "I'm fine." Using her cane, she left the kitchen.

"Stubborn," Anthony muttered.

"I know someone like that." Kaley stood and began clearing the plates off the table.

"Really?" He raised his eyebrows. "You don't have to clear the table."

"Let me help. You cooked."

He nodded. Within twenty minutes, they had the table cleared, leftovers put away, and the dishes were in the dishwasher.

"I need to get home; tomorrow is a work day," Kaley said.

"I wish you'd stay for a bit." He enjoyed being around her.

"I want to, but I have some things to get ready for tomorrow."

There was regret in her voice, and Anthony took that as a good sign. "All right. Let's go tell Gran, and I'll get you home."

Kaley said her goodbyes to Clara, and Anthony guided her out to his vehicle. He wished the drive to Kaley's apartment was longer, but it wasn't. When they arrived, the main door to her building was wide open.

"Stay here," he ordered and jumped out. If there was something going on, he didn't want Kaley caught up in the middle of it. Loud voices reached him before he made it inside. This was not good. He listened to the argument. Sounded like they were arguing over the husband coming home late again. At least it didn't sound like they were trying to kill each other.

He returned and opened the driver's door. "Neighbors are having a fight."

"Oh. Probably apartment two. They've been at it a lot lately." She didn't even seem fazed by his words. He wasn't sure if that was a good thing or not, but he needed to trust her. Kaley opened her door and climbed out.

Anthony took her elbow, and they went in together. He pushed the building door shut, not that it locked. He hadn't been able to find any information on the building owner or management. He needed to know Kaley was safe. At her apartment, she opened the door and waited until he made sure everything was okay.

She stepped inside, and he closed the door, throwing the main dead bolt. "I don't like leaving you here alone."

"It's fine." She hung her purse in the small closet next to the door after she took her cell phone out.

He shook his head. "It's not fine. How violent do they get?" Even though Kaley was down the hall, he could still hear the couple screaming at each other.

"They just yell at each other."

The sound of crashing glass echoed down the hall.

"Occasionally throw things."

Anthony shook his head. He needed to do something. "Would you consider packing a bag and coming back to the house to stay the night?"

Kaley gave him a shy smile as she shook her head. "I'll be fine."

"Where's your van?"

"In a locked garage behind the building."

"Well, at least that's something." Kaley crossed over to him and put her hand on his arm.

"Honestly, Anthony. I'll be fine. This happens all the time. I'm used to it."

"Just because you're used to it doesn't mean it's safe."

"Agreed. Go back and take care of Clara." She unlocked and opened her front door.

"I don't like it."

She shook her head. "If something happens that worries me, I'll call you."

"Call the police first, then me. Promise."

"I promise."

It was the best he was going to get from her at this point. Leaning down, he brushed a kiss over her lips. "We'll talk tomorrow. Early." He shut the door behind him and waited until he heard the dead bolts lock. At least she had more than one.

Once back in his SUV, Anthony sat there. He couldn't make himself leave even though he needed to get back home. He pulled his cell out and called Logan, a police officer he knew from the club.

"Hey, Anthony, what's up?"

"Are you on duty tonight?"

"I am. Is something going on at your grandmother's house?"

"No. It's the apartment building where Kaley lives." Anthony quickly outlined the situation.

"I see. I'll send a car around. There's really not much they can do."

"Just knowing they'll be around to check things out makes me feel better. Now if I could find out who owns this building."

"You might check with Allison, Zeke's girlfriend. She works at the city planning office."

"Great idea. Thanks, Logan. Are you going to make it to the club Saturday night?" Logan's hours weren't always great for him to attend.

"Yes. Finally have a weekend off, and I intend to enjoy it." There were muffled voices.

"I'll let you go. Thanks again for the help." Anthony hung up, feeling a little better about leaving Kaley here. He rolled down his window. No more shouting. He wasn't sure if that was a good thing or not.

As he pulled out of the parking lot, a police car pulled in. Anthony relaxed. Logan was as good as his word. Now he only hoped they were a deterrent and not a match to dynamite.

* * * *

Kaley had just finished checking her email when there was a knock at her door. She frowned as she stood. She wasn't expecting anyone. Quietly, she approached the door and looked out the peephole.

Two officers stood there. Leaving the heavy-duty chain on, she opened the door. "Can I help you?"

"We're just checking on all the tenants, ma'am. Is everything okay?"

"I'm fine. Has something happened?"

86

The officer who had the name Reynolds stitched on his uniform shook his head. "No ma'am just a report of loud voices. We're making sure all the tenants are okay."

Kaley nodded. "Thank you."

"You're welcome, ma'am. Have a good evening." They walked away.

Kaley shut and locked the door. She wondered who had reported the disturbance to the police and why they took it seriously. In this neighborhood, if someone called, it would usually be a day or more before they came out.

It's just how things were. Shutting down her laptop, Kaley got ready for bed. She'd read for a little bit then go to sleep. As she lay in bed, she thought about Anthony wanting to paint her.

His work was fantastic. A painting of her would never compare, but if Anthony really wanted to paint her and could work around her schedule, she might let him.

How would he paint her? Her skin heated, thinking about lying naked on the sofa in the sunroom as he painted. Funny how her thinking about being naked in front of him didn't bother her. After this afternoon, she wanted Anthony. He'd shown her a side of her she never knew was there.

She closed her eyes. Maybe she was wrong to take things this slow. It was time to let herself go. She could be her own woman and let go of her past. And a little flirtation with Anthony would be fun.

Chapter 10

Kaley smiled when she saw Anthony waiting at the front of her apartment building. He'd been here every night this week with dinner for her.

"You don't have to keep doing this," she said, holding her keys in her hand.

"I do." He leaned over and brushed a kiss over her lips.

She was getting frustrated with him doing that. Light kisses, cupping her elbow, arm touches, and holding hands. She enjoyed that he was a very physical person. But lately, she wanted more than light kisses and caresses.

But she didn't know how to get him to move faster. She had been the aggressor in her previous relationships; maybe that needed to change. She put her key in the lobby door, another mystery. When she got home on Wednesday, the apartment manager was handing out new keys to the front door that had been replaced.

The manager didn't look happy about it, but it made Kaley feel a little safer. She opened the door and held it for Anthony. "Something smells good." She couldn't quite place the food.

"Lara was kind enough to make some food for us."

"Doesn't the café close at three?" Kaley unlocked her apartment door and waited until Anthony made his security check.

"It does. She did me a favor." He set a couple of bags in the kitchen. "It will keep for a few more minutes. Go shower and change."

Kaley laughed as she made her way into her bedroom. Anthony had learned her routine and encouraged her to keep it. She took a quick shower and changed into her lounging outfit—a pair of old sweats and a T-shirt. The microwave beeped as she stepped into the living room.

Anthony lifted his head from where he was arranging a variety of food on a platter. "We have beef and chicken empanadas, turkey bagel dogs, and clam chowder." He gestured to the two bowls sitting next to the platter. "And I didn't forget dessert." He grabbed another platter. "For your pleasure, caramel pecan fudge cake, lemon cake, brownies, and cupcakes."

"Goodness, Anthony." She looked over everything. "There's more food than we can eat."

"If I know you, you skipped lunch."

Kaley ducked her head. It was the one argument they had. When she was busy, she didn't eat, and Anthony didn't like it. "It was a busy day," she said softly.

He huffed. "Go sit down, and I'll bring everything in."

"I can help." She reached for the platter with the empanadas and bagel dogs, and he slapped her hand away.

"Go sit."

Dom voice. One that said she better obey or else. Kaley shook her head and went to her small table. It really was more like a bistro table. Barely enough room for the platters, utensils, napkins, and drinks.

She waited while Anthony brought everything in and sat down before she grabbed an empanada. She took a bite. The beef and potatoes filled her taste buds. Kaley hummed, enjoying the spices along with the feeling of being wrapped in comfort.

"Lara is good. Haven't you had her empanadas before?"

Kaley nodded her head. "I have; she's brought them to the club."

"You've never been to her café?"

"No time. She's not open on Sundays."

"You really need to make time for lunch and stop there." He picked up a bagel dog and held it out to her. "Take a bite."

She leaned forward and took a bite, enjoying the crunchiness of the breading around the turkey dog.

"Tell me about your day?"

"Pretty much the same as all the other days this week, grooming dogs and cats."

"I still can't believe you groom cats."

"Cats need to be groomed now and then, but most of them just need sanitary shaves."

"That sounds painful."

"I keep a pair of heavy-duty gloves, but usually, I can sweet-talk them into letting me work on them. Keeping the hair clean around their private areas so they're able to do their business makes it better for the animal and their humans."

Anthony blinked and then laughed. "Those are very polite words."

"What do you expect?" While they had talked kink this week, it was more general than specific. "I can't talk to my clients like we do in private."

"I guess." He picked up the empty soup bowls and platter and carried them into the kitchen. When he returned, he had a fork in his hand. She watched him as he moved his chair closer to her. "What dessert do you want to try first?"

"Where's my fork?"

"You don't get one."

She frowned. What was he up to? "The lemon cake."

Anthony slid the fork into the lemon cake and held the fork up to her lips. Kaley opened her mouth, and he slid it in. A shiver went through her as he pulled the fork from her closed lips.

Sweet and tart lemon overwhelmed her taste buds. Anthony grabbed another piece and put it into his mouth. "So good," he whispered. "Next?"

"Brownie." This time, he picked it up and held it out to her. When she raised her hand to take it, he frowned at her. Lowering her hand, she closed her teeth over the brownie and bit. So good. Fudgy chocolate, not overcooked but not undercooked either.

Anthony lifted the brownie to his mouth and took a bite, all the while holding her gaze. Heat flared in his eyes, and it echoed in Kaley's belly. A man had never fed her like this before.

"Next?"

Kaley shook her head. "That's enough for the moment." She was getting full and very close to begging him to do something more than just feed her. Could she convince him to take it to another level tonight?

"Okay. I'll wrap these up for later." He took the platter into the kitchen. "Do you want me to make you some hot tea?"

"I'm okay, thank you." The man was so thoughtful. She usually had a cup of tea after dinner to help her relax.

Anthony came back into the room and pulled her to her feet and led her over to her sofa. Then he sank onto the cushions.

"I really need a new sofa."

"I don't mind." He put his arm around her shoulders, pulling her to him.

Kaley enjoyed Anthony holding her. He'd done it every night this week. He would hold her after dinner, and they'd chat. She didn't own a TV.

"Have you given more thought to being my model?"

"I have." She tilted her head back and gazed into his blue eyes. "Will you tell me more about what it will involve?"

His eyes lit up. "Mainly having you sit for me in my studio while I sketch you."

"Dressed?" She'd wondered about that.

"Up to you."

Kaley nodded. "How long do you think it will take?"

"It depends on how often you're able to model for me."

"I work pretty much six days a week. As you know, Sunday is usually my day for doing house stuff and making sure my equipment is all ready for the next week."

"But you had time last Sunday."

"I did." Because she'd been motivated to see him again, and there hadn't been that much to do. She took a deep breath. "I'd like to try."

His arm tightened around her shoulders. "Thank you."

"Don't thank me yet. It will have to be on Sundays, and I don't want to interfere with your work with the kids."

"Even just an hour would be great."

Kaley smiled. His face was so animated at this idea. "Maybe after you're done with the kids on Sunday. That would give me time to get all my stuff done and still get home early enough to get ready for Monday."

"Sounds like a plan."

She relaxed against him. She still didn't think she was model material, but she was willing to let Anthony figure that out for himself.

"Would you be open to a scene in the club tomorrow night?"

"I would." It was time. She was ready to move forward, and she trusted Anthony, more than any other man she'd been with. He wouldn't take a scene further than she could handle.

He shifted. "That means I'll leave now and let you get some sleep so you're not so tired tomorrow."

She appreciated his concern, but she'd made sure she would be done by five tomorrow. She stood with him and walked him to the door.

"I'll see you tomorrow."

Anthony drew her into his arms and lowered his head. Kaley didn't hesitate; she kissed him back, her arms going around his neck. For once, he didn't hold back when her tongue touched his.

He pulled her closer. She loved being in his arms. Each night this week, they'd kissed before he left, and each night, her body caught fire in his arms. Tonight, the kiss went on and on, their tongues exploring each other. She stretched her fingers into his hair as his roamed her back.

Maybe she could ask him to stay, but she knew if he did, she'd never get any sleep, and she wanted to be alert and fresh for her scene with him tomorrow. She moaned as he lifted his head.

Anthony leaned his forehead against hers. "You taste so sweet. I don't want to leave." Kaley closed her eyes, then opened them. "But you need to sleep. Tomorrow, my lady." Anthony stepped back, unlocked her apartment door, and left.

She locked up and leaned against the wood. Tomorrow night, she would let her control go. A shiver ran through her veins.

It was the first time she'd do a full scene with him and she wondered how well they would mesh together. Kaley knew she trusted him, but a part of her was apprehensive. She'd never fully scened with anyone in the club, not even during her training. It was a good thing she had bar duty first; it would give her time to talk with some of the other subs.

Chapter 11

Anthony glanced over at the bar where Kaley was working. She'd asked him to not sit at the bar until after nine tonight. At the time, he wondered why. Now he knew. In between serving people, she was talking with several of the subs.

Right now, she was talking with Regina and Crystal. He figured Kaley was a little nervous about tonight. In the past week, they'd talked more about soft and hard limits and about the club itself.

It was interesting how quickly Kaley had settled into their relationship. She allowed him to bring her dinner and told him it made her happy not having to think about food at the end of the day.

She was letting him make a lot of the decisions, but he didn't interfere with her business. That was solidly in her control.

He was at her building every night and cleared her apartment before allowing her to enter. He still hadn't told her about his call to Allison at the city planning office so he could make sure her building was more secure.

There was a sub inside Kaley waiting for the right time to emerge. She was beginning to trust him. He watched her at the bar, laughing as Crystal said something.

"Is there a reason you're not at the bar?" Max asked, clapping him on the shoulder.

"Kaley asked me to wait a bit. She's chatting with some of the subs."

Max glanced at the bar. "I see. You two going to scene tonight?"

"Yes. I think she might be nervous."

"Not unusual. She doesn't have a lot of experience."

"I know." Anthony took a deep breath. "I've been taking her dinner every night this week, and we've chatted. Together, we work."

"If you didn't, I'd be the first one to tell you."

"What?" Anthony stared at Max.

"I see everyone's questionnaires. If a Dom and sub don't seem compatible to me, I'll sit them down and talk with them before there is any play between them."

"Have you ever been wrong?"

Max shook his head. "The only thing I'd be careful with is the knife play. That's a hard limit for Kaley."

"I know." He enjoyed knife play, but it wasn't something that was necessary in his kink life. A lot of subs had knife play as a hard limit, even some of the Doms. He had tried to bring it up this week, and Kaley had shut him down. Maybe once they built more of a relationship, she'd open up to him.

"If you don't mind my asking, what kind of scene do you have planned?"

"Bondage with some impact play." He wouldn't get too deep into the impact play; Kaley agreed to light impact play. "We chatted about it, and I'll go over it again before we start tonight."

"Good. As I said, I think she's in good hands." Max patted his shoulder.

Anthony watched Max walk away. Even beyond the paperwork, the man had an uncanny way of knowing everything about everyone. That's probably what made him so good at running the club. Anthony's watch vibrated. It was nine. He could go to the bar now.

He hesitated. Sierra and Allyson were at the bar chatting with Kaley. Then Kaley looked up, and their gazes clashed. Her cheeks turned pink. The other two women turned and smiled at him. Anthony waved to both.

The women turned back around, said something, then patted Kaley's hand before leaving the bar. Anthony sauntered over and sat on one of the now vacant stools.

"Drink?" Kaley asked.

"I'm good. You okay?"

"Fine. Why?"

"You looked a little flustered while talking to Sierra and Allyson."

This time the flush wasn't contained to her cheeks. It started at her chest and spread up. "Not going to discuss it."

"No problem. Noah takes over at ten, right?"

"Yes." She glanced to her left. "Be right back."

Anthony kept his gaze on her when she walked to the other end of the bar and served a man who identified as a Dom. Anthony remembered he'd said his name was Ward. She placed the glass in front of him and poured some juice. Ward said something, and she shook her head.

The next thing Anthony knew, the self-professed Dom grabbed Kaley's wrist. Anthony surged to his feet.

"Red." Kaley's voice was clear and strong. Colby and Zeke were there before Anthony could take a step. Ward released Kaley and held his hands up. Anthony approached the group.

"Are you okay, Kaley?" Colby asked, watching carefully as she rubbed her wrist.

"I am now, Sir." Anthony stepped up to Colby's left. Kaley's gaze met his. She wasn't fine. He could see the fear in her eyes. "Zeke, would you get Noah?"

Zeke nodded.

"She has a white wristband on," Ward muttered.

"White means novice. It doesn't mean you can put your hands on her without permission," Colby said.

Anthony ignored Ward and held his hand out to Kaley. She placed her hand in his, and he examined her wrist.

"I'm okay," she whispered. He rubbed the red spot on her wrist.

"What's going on?" Noah asked.

"Can you take over a little early?" Anthony asked.

"Sure." Noah frowned when he saw Anthony rubbing Kaley's wrist. "Are you okay, Kaley?"

She sighed. "I'm fine, and I can finish out my shift." Anthony stared at her, and she sighed again. "Honestly, you Doms need to take it down a notch."

"Never," Anthony muttered.

"Let's go have a chat, Ward." Colby gestured for Ward to walk away.

"Whatever." Ward left with Colby, Zeke, and Noah following. Within a minute, Max and Jordan joined them.

"Hey, Kaley. Can I get some water, please," Regina yelled from the other end of the bar.

"Coming right up." She slipped her hand from his and moved down the bar. Anthony's gaze never left her as she handed two bottles of water to Regina, then started checking in with the others sitting at the bar.

Anthony glanced over to where the men stood. Ward was gesturing with his hands, and Max was shaking his head. Then Max turned and approached Anthony. "Before I take any action, did you see him grab Kaley?"

"Yes."

"Without her permission?"

"Yes." Anthony's fingers curled into his palms.

"Anyone else?"

Several of the men spoke up, saying Kaley was just pouring Ward a drink when he grabbed her. Max nodded. "Thank you all." He looked back at Anthony. "I need to talk to Kaley."

"I want to stay with her."

"Of course." Noah walked behind the bar and touched Kaley on the shoulder. There was brief conversation; she nodded and walked toward Max.

"Master Max." Her voice was quiet.

"Kaley. Tell me what happened, please."

Her gaze flitted to Anthony then back to Max. "I poured the Dom a glass of juice. As I was turning away, he grabbed my wrist, and I called red."

"Did he release you right away?"

"I'm not sure. I know he let go when Colby and Zeke ran up."

"That's what I wanted to know." Max looked at Anthony. "Take care of her." Max left.

"I can take care of myself," she muttered. Max turned around and gave her a hard look before going back to where Colby, Zeke, Jordan, and Ward stood.

"Come on, sweetheart. Let's go sit down and chat." He slipped his arm around her waist.

"You know, once in a while, you Doms need to listen."

"We are always listening and sometimes to more than the words you say." He guided her across the room to an empty sofa and gestured for her to sit down.

"I'm being serious." She flopped down and crossed her arms over her chest. "He startled me; that was all."

"There was fear in your eyes." He wasn't going to let her downplay what had happened.

"I wasn't scared. Startled was all."

"Let me ask this question. Why did you call the club safe word?"

"Because he was touching me without permission, and that's the rule."

She didn't hesitate, and it made him smile. "And if he hadn't let you go?"

"I know enough to protect myself. Colby and Zeke were there, and you weren't far behind. Plus there were three other Doms at the bar. Someone would have intervened."

For the first time since Ward grabbed her, Anthony could breathe. "You're right. I'm glad you called your safe word."

She let out a breath and glanced over his shoulder. "What is Master Max going to do?"

"I don't know." Anthony was aware it wasn't Ward's first incident with the subs. "Are you okay talking about our scene tonight?"

Her eyes brightened. "Yes."

"We talked earlier in the week. And that night I took your wrists in my hand and held you against the wall of your apartment, you like being restrained."

"Oh yes. It was exciting." She squirmed in her seat.

"I've got one of the bondage stages for us." She nodded. "I'm going to restrain you and then use some impact toys on you."

"What kind, Sir?" Her breathing had deepened.

"A light flogger and a padded paddle. You'll feel them both, but nothing that will last beyond a few minutes."

"May I see the toys?"

"Of course. Be right back." He stood and crossed over to the cubbies that held the Doms' bags. He grabbed his and made his way back to Kaley. Unzipping the bag, he pulled out a rabbit flogger and the paddle.

Her eyes widened, and she held out a trembling hand. Anthony laid the flogger in her palm. Her fingers curled around the handle, and she held it up so the tails hung down. With her free hand, she ran her fingers over the fur.

"The rabbit flogger is good for a beginner. It will be soft and sensual. You'll feel a little thud, but nothing hard."

"I understand, Sir." She handed him the flogger, and he put the paddle in her hand.
"It's heavier, Sir."

"Yes. Soft fur on one side and leather on the other." He kept his gaze on her. While her hands trembled, her breathing was slightly faster, and her skin turned pink.

"You'll only use the fur side, Sir?"

"Yes. Tonight is for you to get used to impact play."

"I see, Sir." Her voice was soft.

Anthony squatted down so he could watch her eyes, expression, and other subtle cues. Her eyes were clear, shoulders relaxed, and her expression curious. "It won't be a long scene. I'll start with the rabbit flogger, then the paddle."

Kaley took a deep breath and let it out slowly. She seemed to be assessing his every move. "May I keep my shorts on? What will that do, Sir?"

"The sensations will be dulled by your clothing, but it's up to you. I want you to feel as comfortable as possible." He believed his words. Kaley was new to the lifestyle, and while he'd never trained a sub, he wanted to with her.

"If I…" She glanced away. Anthony cupped her chin, and her gaze collided with his. She swallowed. "I have a thong on underneath my shorts; can I keep that on and lose the shorts, Sir?"

Her body flushed further, and he couldn't suppress a smile. "That is acceptable." He was surprised at her request. She'd seemed reluctant before now to shed her clothes.

"Okay. I can do this, Sir."

"I'm sure you can." He placed the two impact items back in his bag. "I have the bondage area reserved for us at ten." One of the dungeon monitors would signal him when it was time. "Until then…" He zipped his bag shut and sat down next to Kaley. "Tell me how you're feeling."

She titled her head. "I'm not sure what you mean, Sir."

"Are you still upset that Ward grabbed you?" If she was, then their scene could wait.

"No, Sir." Her gaze skidded away again. Anthony waited in silence until she looked at him.

Anthony nodded. "I'm proud of you for using your safe word. Some subs might not."

"No man touches me without permission, Sir."

"Well then, it's a good thing I have your permission."

She ducked her head. "You will always have my permission, Sir."

Her trust sent a wave of delight through him. They hadn't known each other very long, but they were connected. "Thank you for your trust." Anthony cupped her cheek. "I will not abuse it."

"What else will happen in our scene, Sir."

"Now, if I told you everything, you couldn't anticipate our scene, but these are the only two impact toys I will be using." He couldn't help that he wanted to see how far he could go tonight. Not that he'd violate a hard limit. Her soft limits were restricted as well, but he could talk to her and touch her, and he planned to do a lot of touching.

Jordan waved at him. "Time, sweetheart." He stood, pulled her to her feet, then picked up his bag. Hand in hand, they walked to the bondage stage. This was one of four. He was using the one with the bondage horse.

Kaley would be able to rest her body against the soft leather, her legs supported by the sides. He didn't want her to get tired their first time in a scene. She removed her shorts and walked over to the spanking horse.

Anthony helped her onto the equipment. "Will it bother you if I restrain you?"

She looked over her shoulder at him. "Green, Sir."

He ran his fingers over her pale skin before doing up the restraints and making sure they didn't cut off her circulation. "I'm going to warm you up a little bit."

"Yes, Sir."

Chapter 12

Kaley took a deep breath as her heart pounded. This was her first scene with Anthony. Well, technically, they did one a few weeks ago, but that was just his hands on her body. This was so much more.

Excitement mixed with fear of the unknown flooded her veins. Here she was on the spanking horse. Her wrists and ankles restrained and her butt in the air. Wasn't this what she wanted? To understand and learn about these desires? She did.

Forcing herself to breathe in and out, she waited. The longer she waited, the more anticipation built in her body, then Anthony ran his hand over her ass, and she jumped.

"Easy, sweetheart," he murmured, caressing her butt. Then gave it a light slap.

A little sting, then heat. Heat flowed through her body, making her squirm with desire. Who knew spanking could elicit that? While they'd touched and kissed over these past few weeks, there had been nothing like this. Another slap. Nerve endings she never knew existed woke up and tingled. She opened her mouth to get more air into her lungs.

"Nice," Anthony whispered, running his hands over her ass again before a harder smack.

"Oh my." The words slipped from her lips. It wasn't that it hurt; instead, it sent shock waves through her body and caused her pussy to clench.

After a few minutes—or was it longer—Anthony stopped and rubbed her ass again. The coolness of his hand against her skin felt good. "How are you doing?"

"Green, Sir." She wondered what was coming next. His hand left her, and she turned her head; he was out of her range of vision. Okay then, it was going to be a surprise.

His fingers trailed over her ass once again. "Let's try something a little bit heavier." Kaley tensed. "Don't tense up, sweetheart."

"Sorry, Sir."

"It's okay." His lips pressed against her spine before slipping away. She heard a slight whoosh sound, and the tails of the rabbit flogger struck her ass.

"Ahhhh." Not a bad sting, but… How did she feel? It was heavier, that was for sure, but her body absorbed the impact like it was nothing. Another one followed the first. If a spanking worked all her nerves, the rabbit flogger woke her desire.

Her clit tingled. Her nipples tightened and were rubbing against the leather of the equipment.

"Be still."

She froze. "Yes, Sir."

Another swat. Kaley closed her eyes, letting the sensations flow through her body. Anthony rubbed her ass again, then started flogging her.

Kaley wasn't sure how to explain it. With each swat, she relaxed more and more, even raised her ass to Anthony. Was this what it meant to give over control to a Dom? A crazy euphoria ran through her body.

"How are we, sweetheart?" Anthony's husky voice penetrated the fog in her brain.

"Green, Sir." Her words were slightly slurred. She wondered about that.

"I bet you are." Anthony began undoing the restraints, and she wondered why. The next thing she knew, he was putting a blanket over her and picking her up.

"Why do I feel so…noodley?"

"Noodley?" There was amusement in his voice.

"Limp." She was having trouble coming up with the right words.

"Because, sweetheart, you're floating on a cloud."

"That sounds nice." Kaley closed her eyes and let herself go lax against Anthony. He'd take care of her.

* * * *

Anthony tightened his hold around Kaley. She had no clue what was going on. She was somewhere between total bliss and what seemed to be subspace. He'd have to be very careful with Kaley if she went into subspace so easily. But he also suspected this was the first time she really let go of everything. He was honored it was with him.

Finding an empty spot in the aftercare area, he sat and cradled Kaley in his lap. He'd never seen her so relaxed. Usually, she was on guard for something—he didn't know what—but he suspected she never truly relaxed. Even when sleeping.

Maybe they needed to discuss why she lived where she lived. It wasn't exactly one of the safest areas. He wanted, no, needed her to be safe. Anthony glanced up as Jordan approached him.

"How is she?" he asked, handing Anthony a bottle of water.

"She's still out of it."

Jordan nodded. "Okay if I clean up the area and put your things away?"

"Are you sure? I can do it."

"Stay with Kaley. It's no big deal."

"Thanks."

Jordan walked away. This was another reason he enjoyed Wicked Sanctuary. Everyone looked out for everyone else, especially Max, Jordan, and Damon. Those three had built one hell of a club.

Anthony relaxed against the sofa and glanced down at Kaley. Her eyes were still closed, her breathing steady and even. Good. She was going to come down slowly, which maybe wasn't a bad thing. He didn't mind sitting there holding her.

About thirty minutes later, she stirred. Anthony looked down as she raised her lashes. Her eyes were clear.

"What happened?"

"What's the last thing you remember?" he asked.

"You were using the rabbit flogger on me. Did we get to the paddle?"

"No to the paddle. You zoned out on me."

"I did? I'm so sorry." She shifted in his arms and started to sit up. Anthony tightened his hold.

"Stay still." Using his free hand, he brushed a strand of her dark red hair off her face. "There's nothing to be sorry about. It wasn't something I expected, but you let your control go, and by doing that, you allowed yourself to relax and feel. Your trust in me is humbling."

"Oh." She blinked. "I had no idea it could be like that."

"You are new to the lifestyle." He shifted so she could sit up a little bit more. "How are you feeling?"

"Pretty good. My ass is still tingling, but otherwise, pretty energized."

He nodded. How did he approach her about this next part. "I know you don't have work tomorrow, and since you were close to or in subspace, I don't feel good about leaving you alone tonight."

"Why?"

"You could have subdrop. You were and probably still are on an endorphin high. When you come down, it's better not to be alone." He wasn't going to leave her alone tonight.

"I can't stay at your grandmother's house."

"We can stay at my place."

"Your grandmother?"

"She has a friend spending the night, so she's fine." It was sheer luck Gran's friend was visiting. Kaley eyes narrowed as she stared at him. "I didn't plan it. I swear."

Soft laughter was music to his ears. "I'm pretty sure there was no way for you to know how I was going to react. I've been in the club long enough to know that much."

Anthony leaned down and kissed her temple. "Then you'll spend the night?"

"I should say no." She put her fingers against his mouth when he opened it to speak. "It makes sense for me to be with you tonight. I honestly don't know what I'm feeling."

He tightened his arms around her. "I'm here for you." And he was. Kaley was his. Well, maybe it was too early to think that, but his heart disagreed.

Chapter 13

Kaley struggled to wake up. Wait a second? Eyes popping open, she saw Anthony's arm and not the blanket she'd been expecting. And the events of last night came rushing back.

Ward grabbing her, the scene she and Anthony had, him holding her, and her agreeing to spend the night with him. Tears stung her eyes, and she forced herself to breathe. There was nothing wrong with what they'd done, so why did she feel all weepy? She wasn't one who cried at a drop of a hat.

"Sweetheart?" His soft voice had her breath catching.

"I…" Oh hell, tears started falling, and she had no idea why.

"Easy." Anthony gathered her into his arms. "You're okay. You're experiencing subdrop, one of the possible aftereffects of achieving subspace."

"What?" She could barely get the word out.

"Remember I told you about this last night."

She nodded. They had talked about it, but… She hated crying.

"Some women cry afterward; others have no aftereffects or feel a little off or depressed. I've heard its normal."

"You've never been around subdrop before?" She sniffled.

"I haven't." Anthony leaned over and grabbed something off the nightstand. When he faced her, he dropped a small box of tissues in her lap.

"Thank you." She took several, wiped her tears, and blew her nose. "I'm not a crier."

"It doesn't matter to me if you are or not. Just lay here and let yourself be. This will pass." He tightened his arms around her and urged her head to his shoulder.

"It better pass fast," she grumbled, but she was already feeling better snuggled up against Anthony's warm body with his arms around her. Safe. She remembered him carrying her from the club to his vehicle, then from the vehicle into his home and putting her to bed. And that was about it. Oh crap. She stiffened.

"What is worrying you?"

"How did you know I was worried? Never mind, Doms can read minds."

He chuckled. "Not really."

"Did you undress me?"

"I only removed your sports bra; you still have your thong on." He cupped her chin and tilted her head until their gazes met. "I didn't want you to be uncomfortable."

She swallowed, afraid to move. "And you?" A blush crept from her chest into her cheeks.

"I have underwear on." He grinned at her. "Although I can take them off if you'd like."

Kaley shook her head. "As much as I'd like that, today isn't the day for it." They'd hadn't gone much beyond light touching and kissing, no real intimacy. She rolled her eyes.

"I saw that eye roll; what does that mean?"

"Nothing." She lowered her gaze. "I need to get up." She wiggled against his hold. "Mother nature is calling."

Anthony released her, but instead of lounging in bed as she expected, he got up and crossed over to her when she sat up. There wasn't an ounce of fat on this man, but she already knew that. Seeing him in a pair of black boxers and, *wham*, her heart pounded, and her mouth watered. Maybe she was more ready to be intimate than she thought. "Don't move too fast," he said as she stood.

"I'm okay." Her tears had disappeared, but her knees were a little wobbly. "Bathroom."

"Over there." He pointed to the slightly open door across the room.

Carefully, Kaley put one leg in front of the other. Her knees held. She pushed open the bathroom door and then shut it behind her. Once she'd used the facilities, she stepped up to the sink. Lord, her hair was a mess, and her make up smeared.

This is what Anthony saw, yet he didn't run screaming or say a word. Kaley blew out a breath, washed her hands, and wondered if she could clean up. "Anthony."

"Yes." His voice was strong and right outside the door. "Are you okay?"

"I'm fine. Do you by chance have an extra toothbrush? Also, I'd like a wash cloth to clean my face."

"Certainly. Wash cloths and extra towels are in the second drawer on your left. Extra toothbrushes are in the drawer above that. Would you like some coffee?"

"Coffee sounds wonderful, thank you." She found the items right where he said they would be. Did he have overnight guests often? She shut her thoughts down; they both had pasts. After she washed her face, she brushed her teeth. It wasn't until that moment that she realized she'd been walking about with her breasts bouncing around for all the world, well, for Anthony to see.

"Smart, Kaley." She grabbed one of the bath towels from the drawer and wrapped it around her body, then opened the bedroom door. It was empty, and she spied her bag from the club, sitting on the chair.

Wanting to be quiet, she tiptoed over to her bag and opened it. Thank goodness she'd thought to pack another pair of underwear. She quickly dressed, then went to look for Anthony. She stopped as she left the bedroom to look around. This was his place.

The high ceiling showed the exposed wood structure, and there was lots of light. The family room held a love seat and a recliner, not to mention a big ass TV mounted on the wall. There was a small dining room with a table and chairs.

"Oh, you got dressed."

She glanced up to see Anthony standing in another doorway that she assumed led to the kitchen. "I did." Moving toward him, she glanced up and saw the overhead loft and windows. That's where the light was coming from.

"Too bad." He held a mug out to her. The twinkle of mischief in his eyes sent a shaft of longing through her body.

She fought it back and ignored his comment. Kaley curled her fingers around the cup, blew on the contents, then took a sip. "How did you know how I took my coffee?"

"Did I get it right?"

"It's perfect. Answer the question." He liked to dodge her questions at times.

"I paid attention when we had breakfast together with Gran. A splash of milk and one sugar."

"Observant." That's probably what made him a good Dom. It was one thing she had noticed about most of the Doms at Wicked Sanctuary: they were very good at people watching.

"I am." He took a sip from his own mug. "Go sit down at the table, and I'll get us some breakfast."

"Coffee is fine." She wasn't sure she could eat anything yet.

Anthony frowned. "You should eat."

Kaley sat, and he followed. There was concern written on his face. "I will, just not at the moment." Her tummy wasn't exactly calm at the moment, and she didn't know why. She took another sip of her coffee.

They sat there in silence for a few minutes, just having their coffee. "This is a very nice place," she said, trying to push away the awkward feeling churning inside her.

"Thank you. I can give you the grand tour later."

"I really should get home. I've got things to do, and you have art class with the kids."

"I do. And this afternoon, you're modeling for me."

Kaley closed her eyes. She'd forgotten about that. "I guess I am."

A warm hand covered hers where it lay on the table. "Do you need more time?"

Her heart turned over. This man was always thinking of her. "I'll be fine. Just remember: I'm not model material."

He shook his head. "You're fine. How about some toast with jam before I take you home?"

"All right." There was determination to feed her before he took her home written all over him. Toast was a good choice.

* * * *

Kaley was barely breathing when she entered the sunroom with Anthony. Her stomach flittered with a thousand butterflies. She'd gone home and completed her work, shaved, and showered to be fresh for this.

"Is what I'm wearing okay?" She'd dressed in a pair of her favorite yoga pants and a soft t-shirt.

"Perfect." Anthony pulled a chair over close to the sofa, then placed a small table with his sketch pad and pencils. "Come here."

His voice was soft, but it didn't calm her anxiety. Why was she so nervous? It was just Anthony.

"I want you to lie down on the sofa, please."

Kaley blew out a breath and did as he asked.

"Oh, Kaley." Anthony walked over to her. "Does this bother you that much?"

"I don't know. Why?"

"You're stiff as a board." He walked away and music filled the room. A soft instrumental of some sort. Anthony returned to her side. "Close your eyes."

She did as he asked, and immediately, her heart raced.

"Deep breath in and let it out." Kaley did this several times at his direction. Her heart slowed to normal, and her muscles relaxed. "That's it. Now, turn slightly on your side to face me." Keeping her eyes closed, she did what he said. "Good girl. Now one arm under your head on the pillows."

Once she was in position, she opened her eyes. Anthony was sitting in the chair with the sketch pad resting in his lap, his forehead wrinkled in concentration.

"If your arm falls asleep or you feel like you need to move, let me know."

"All right." She let the soft music flow over her as she stared at this complex man sketching her.

* * * *

Anthony's fingers flew over his sketch pad. It didn't matter that Kaley was fully dressed; his mind supplied what he'd seen this morning. Her pert breasts, flat belly, and curvy ass. She was perfect.

He filled one sheet after another. Maybe one day she'd allow him to sketch her nude, but for right now, he was happy. His muse was happy. He couldn't wait to turn his sketches into paintings.

A twinge of unease went through him. In any public pictures, she would be fully clothed, but for him, she would be gloriously naked. He ran his pencil over the paper, catching the unique curve of her jaw, the sensual look on her face.

Oh yes, it was sensual. Her gaze was unfocused and her body relaxed. That's what he wanted. That piece of her she kept under wraps. The real Kaley who hid herself for reasons he had yet to find out.

"Anthony." Her soft voice had him lifting his head.

"Yes, sweetheart."

"Sorry, but I need to move."

"Of course." He closed his sketch book and set it aside before moving to the sofa to help her into a seated position.

Kaley shook out her arm and flexed her fingers. He frowned. "You should have said something earlier." He took her arm and rubbed it gently.

"It was fine until a few minutes ago when I realized my arm was falling asleep. I hated to disturb you. You had a look of fierce concentration."

"I get that way." He glanced down at his watch. His eyes widened. "You sat that way for two hours without moving."

"It was nice." She smiled. "I don't think I've ever relaxed like that in my life except maybe when I'm sleeping."

"You are a treasure." He cupped her chin and kissed her. Anthony deepened the kiss as she turned toward him.

"Ah, excuse me."

Anthony lifted his head to see is grandmother standing in the doorway. "Hey, Gran, what do you need?"

"Sorry to interrupt. Nugget needs to go out, and you mentioned you wanted to have Kaley home by five; it's after that now."

"Thanks, Gran. I'll be right there." His grandmother left, and he turned back to Kaley.

Her cheeks were flushed.

"Sorry to break this up. Stay for dinner?"

Kaley shook her head. "I have to put gas in the van tonight and check email to make sure there are no cancellations."

Anthony rested his forehead against hers, staring into her eyes. "All right." He wanted to convince her to stay, but she did have a job. He stood and then helped her to her feet. "Let me take Nugget out right quick, then I'll take you home."

"Okay. I am sorry, Anthony."

"For what?"

"For needing to leave."

He grinned. "We'll have our time together soon." Another kiss and he pulled back before his body went into overdrive. Yes, he wanted her in his bed and in his life. But it wouldn't happen tonight. They had time.

Chapter 14

"Hi there, beautiful," Anthony said the next Saturday night at the club.

"Handsome," Kaley quipped back with a smile. The week had been a good one. She sat for Anthony on Sunday. It was fascinating to watch him work. The concentration on his face, the way his hand flew over the sketch pad, and the passion in his eyes.

She'd learned a lot about him this week. The loft in his house was his studio, but also where he kept his knives. Kaley shivered. She avoided that area even when Anthony asked her if she wanted to see them. Out of habit, she rubbed right below her ribcage.

Enough. It was a long time ago, and Anthony wasn't the person who hurt her. Not that she would play with knives, nope that was out of the question.

"Do you want to scene tonight?" he asked her.

"If you'd like." All week, again, he was at her apartment waiting with food when she got home. She tried to convince him to stop, but he wouldn't listen. Each night, he left her with a scorching kiss and erotic dreams. Her frustration level was getting high that he wasn't listening to her.

Kaley almost laughed. She hadn't had sex in a couple of years due to her work schedule and never finding a man she wanted in her bed. Now she was feeling impatient because Anthony heard her when she said she wanted to go slow. She was a mass of contradictions.

"I would like." Anthony picked up her hand. "I'm going to check with Max and see if I can get the area I want."

Kaley stiffened.

"Within boundaries. I might push your soft limits a bit, but I won't go over. Promise. Do you trust me?"

Her shoulders dropped. "Yes." She did and had told him that before.

"Then remember: I will follow your limits." He squeezed her hand before letting go and sliding off the stool. "Be back in a minute."

She watched him walk away, enjoying the view of his body's fluid movements as he walked. Damn, that man was built. She wasn't surprised. A member called her name, and she went to get their order. It was going to be a long shift.

* * * *

Anthony grinned as he headed over to speak to Max. He wondered if she was as frustrated as he was. Lately she had been giving off signals she wanted more and was ready to move forward. The frustration was his own fault. He wanted to take his time with her. He was enjoying finding out little things about her. She didn't like spicy food, never watched TV, read local news on the computer, and loved to read.

Oh, and she didn't like knives. Knife play was a hard limit with her, and he understood. He'd seen the fear in her eyes when he showed her his loft on Wednesday. She had avoided the area where the knives were. She'd glanced at the table once, then adverted her eyes, apparently to make sure not to look at them again. There was something there. He would ask her about it when the time felt right. And maybe in a few years, when they were more comfortable with each other, and had talked more about it, he would consider pushing that limit.

Max was talking with another Dom, so Anthony waited several feet away.

"Anthony," Max said as the other Dom walked away.

"Evening, Max. I was wondering if the garden is empty tonight?"

"It is, for once. What time do you want it?"

"Ten, when Kaley finishes with her bar shift."

"You got it. I'll post the sign, and you should be fine."

"Thanks." Anthony turned away. Tonight would be fun.

* * * *

"The garden?" Kaley's voice held disbelief.

"Yes."

Kaley shook her head. "I thought that was only for parties." She didn't remember ever seeing it for private use, but then she'd only been a member a few months.

"Max does allow private use. And tonight, it's ours."

Anthony put his arm around her waist, opened the door, and led her out. Kaley was in her normal sports bra and boy shorts, along with flat shoes. They were lucky; today had been a scorcher and the night air was still warm. He dropped his bag by the door. "Here are the rules for tonight." He turned her to face him. "You have thirty minutes to make it to the clearing on the other side of the garden."

"There has to be more than that." Kaley was suspicious. She hadn't been in the garden, but she'd heard some of the subs talk about it.

"If you make it to the clearing without me catching you, you win. But if I catch you, I win."

"And what do I win?"

"Anything you want."

She tilted her head and stared at him. "If you win?"

Fire burned in his gaze. "Anything I want."

"Within my limits."

He nodded. She was still suspicious, but how hard could this be? "You're on."

Anthony pulled a stop watch out of his bag. "Thirty minutes. Go."

She turned and jogged to the entrance and slipped into the garden.

* * * *

Kaley blew out a breath. She had no clue how much time had passed. Anthony had tricked her. The hedges were over six feet tall, and she had no idea where she was in the garden. No one had mentioned it was a maze.

She walked straight to an open area from which there were two ways to go. She tried the first one and ended up in another open area, but not out of the hedges. This was so unfair. She should have expected that from Master Max and the other Doms. They always stacked the odds in their favor.

A rustling sound had her moving to her right. She had to come out on the other side soon. Frustration hit her in the gut when she came to another choice. Damn. Right or left? She'd been staying right, but maybe it was time to go left.

More rustling sounds. It wasn't the wind, since it was calm and warm tonight. Was it Anthony? Or something else? A shiver chased up her spine. She liked animals, but the club was near the woods, and it was highly possible wildlife had found the garden.

She glanced around. While there was light, it was trail lights. Her heart picked up speed as the rustling came closer. Think! Kaley screamed when Anthony appeared in front of her.

"Gotcha." He pulled her into his arms.

"You fiend." She punched his shoulder. "You scared me."

He had the nerve to laugh. Oh this man liked to play, did he? Well, she'd show him how playful she could be.

"Let me go." She squirmed in his hold.

"I won."

"You cheated."

"That's a serious charge. What is your proof?"

Kaley couldn't stop the giggle that bubbled up and escaped. Anthony looked so serious. He frowned at her. Without thought, she twisted out of his hold and ran.

"I'm coming for you," Anthony yelled.

She laughed and kept running, ducking in and around some of the hedges. He might have won the first round, but she could outsmart him, right? She sent a prayer heavenward and kept running.

After a few minutes, she stopped and listened. She couldn't hear anything but her own breathing. That wasn't good. Looking up at the night sky, she tried to figure out her position. Darn, she'd never been very good at science in school.

Maybe a better strategy would be to head back to the club rather than farther into the garden. Okay, she turned to the left. Was that the club? She saw a faint outline in the distance and headed in that direction.

Yes! She was right. Exiting the hedges, she saw the door to the club.

"Mine." Anthony captured her around her waist and hauled her to him.

"Not fair."

He laughed, tossed her over his shoulder, and carried her away from the door. She struggled, but not too hard. This was too much fun. "Oh, Sir, what will you do with me?" The giggle that escaped her lips made a mockery of her words.

"Whatever I want."

They reached one of the clearings, and he set her on her feet. There were fairy lights in the trees and, in the center of the clearing, a covered mattress with pillows and blankets. Of course, his toy bag sat off to the side.

"Someone has been busy."

"I had to keep busy while you found your way through."

"Sneaky Dom."

"Don't you forget it." He drew her into his arms. Anthony lowered his head and captured her lips.

Kaley sighed and sank into his kiss. Anthony had been so careful with her these last few weeks, not moving too fast. She was ready for the next step, especially after their impact play scene.

"I lose myself in your kisses," he whispered against her lips. Capturing her hand, he led her over to the mattress. "Lie down."

His deep voice sent a shiver of anticipation through her veins. "Yes, Sir." The sheets were soft against her skin as she laid down

"I'm going to blindfold you." He held up a black cloth.

"Yes, Sir." Anthony knelt and tied it around her head, and a tremor went through her body.

"Okay, sweetheart?"

"Green, Sir." And she was. Even without her sight, her body was on alert to see what he would do next. Kaley relaxed against the mattress and listened.

The call of a bird echoed in the clearing, Anthony's movements carried to her ears, and she waited. She had no idea what he had in his bag, and the mystery increased her anticipation.

He touched her wrist, and she jumped. "Easy, sweetie."

Kaley settled down and focused on what Anthony was doing. Furry cuffs were wrapped around her wrists and ankles, then she was bound. Not that she minded; bondage was kind of fun.

"Well, darn. How do you feel about your clothing, sweetheart?"

"What do you mean?" She had on her normal sports bra and boy shorts.

"I want you naked."

"Oh." How did she feel about that? "What if someone comes out into the garden?" Was she ready to be naked in front of other club members? People she knew?

"No one will. Trust me to protect you."

"Yes, Sir." Her voice was a little shaky.

"I don't want you to panic. I'm going to cut your clothes off of you."

She nodded, but when the coldness of steel touched her skin, she stiffened… "Red!"

The blindfold was whipped away and the restraints released. Anthony lifted her into a seated position with concern on his face. "Kaley?"

The nightmare of a knife flashed in front of her eyes. The coldness of it as it sliced through her skin. An icy shiver slipped over her spine, and her whole body shook. She had to get away, claw her way out. He was near. Her gut clenched. She could only stare as the garden faded, and she was thrown back to a dark place.

Chapter 15

"What the fuck?" Anthony held Kaley's arms to her side to prevent her from hitting him or hurting herself. She was unresponsive when he called her name. She'd been with him until he touched her with the scissors to cut her bra strap. When she yelled red, his heart stopped.

He grabbed a blanket and pulled it over her. "Kaley, honey, talk to me." No response. She'd calmed down, but her eyes stared at some spot over his shoulder. Getting to his knees, he managed to get her into his arms with the blanket around her, and rose to his feet.

Walking quickly, he made his way the entrance to the club. He opened the door and looked around for Max or one of the other Doms. He had no experience with this, and he was worried.

"What's wrong?" Jordan asked, walking up to him.

"Kaley called her safe word and then went…kind of catatonic." Anthony's heart pounded. What had he done wrong?

"Got it. Come on." Jordan cleared a path to one of the private rooms and opened the door for him. "Best advice right now, lay on the bed with her and keep talking to her. Let me get the first aid kit and Regina."

Anthony nodded and strode into the room. Once he had them on the bed, he started talking to Kaley.

"Come on, sweetheart," he said. "Whatever happened, I'm sorry. We can talk this through; just come back to me." He rubbed her arms and rocked her gently. Anthony was fighting against panicking.

Jordan walked back in with Regina. "Tell me exactly what happened," Regina said.

Anthony remembered Regina was a nurse. He relayed what he'd done and what happened. Regina frowned and checked Kaley's pulse.

"I think you hit a trigger." Regina straightened.

"Trigger?" Anthony had heard about triggers. "How could I have prevented it?"

"You couldn't," Regina said. "You had no idea it existed."

"What do I do now?" Anthony was at a loss.

"Sit here with her. She'll come around." Regina glanced at Jordan.

"I'll let the others know." He nodded to Regina, who left the room. "I'll be sitting outside the door, so if you need anything, holler."

"Thanks, Jordan. I've never seen anything like this. It's way past scary."

"I know." Jordan put his hand on Anthony's shoulder. "She'll come around soon, and just know that she might not talk about it."

Anthony nodded. He shifted and kissed Kaley's cheek. "Come back to me, sweetheart."

* * * *

Kaley snuggled into the warmth of the body holding her. Wait a second? Her eyes opened. She was inside, but she'd been in the garden. Tilting her head back, Anthony looked down at her with concern written all over his face.

"There's my Kaley," he whispered.

She tried to sit up, but he tightened his arms around her.

"Relax. How do you feel?"

"Tired. I'm not sure why, except you chased me around the garden." She glanced around and realized they were in a private room. "When did we come inside the club?"

"What do you last remember?" His voice was soft, but there was a twinge of worry there.

"We were in the clearing. I was on the bed, you put a blindfold on me, restrained me, then talked about how you forgot to remove my clothes and..." Blackness filled her mind. "I don't remember."

"Anything?"

"Nothing." She frowned. "What happened?"

"Just a minute." Anthony shifted. "Jordan."

"Hey." Jordan stuck his head in the room. "Oh good, you're awake."

"Yes." She shivered. Anthony tightened his hold on her.

Jordan grabbed one of the blankets sitting on the chair, shook it open, and draped it over her. "Thank you." Why was she so cold?

"No problem." Jordan looked at Anthony. "What do you need?"

"Would you ask Regina to come in. Kaley doesn't remember what happened."

Jordan nodded and left.

"I'm fine." Another shiver racked her body.

"I want Regina to check you out."

She opened her mouth.

"It's not up for negotiation. You've been out of it for two hours."

"What?" Two hours. "You mean I've been asleep for that long?" That's what he had to mean. Anthony shook his head, but didn't say anything.

Jordan returned with Regina.

"Glad to see you awake," Regina said, reaching down and putting her fingers on Kaley's wrist. "A little fast, but steady. How do you feel?"

"A little cold but otherwise okay," Kaley said.

"She doesn't remember calling her safe word," Anthony said.

Regina frowned. "What's the last thing you do remember?"

"As I told Anthony, I remember being restrained and him telling me he forgot to take my clothes off, and that's it. A total blank after that until I woke up here in his arms."

Anthony's arms tightened around her, and Kaley snuggled against him. How could she forget two hours? Let alone saying her safe word.

"I see." Regina checked her eyes, then checked her body.

"What are you looking for?" Kaley asked.

"Any bites or anything that might have caused an adverse reaction. I didn't find any earlier, but that doesn't mean something won't show up now."

"Earlier?" Kaley was confused.

"Yes." Regina straightened. "When Anthony brought you in, Master Jordan asked me to check you out. I still don't see anything, and since you're awake and alert, and your color is good, I'm going with my initial thought."

"Which was?" Confused, Kaley needed to understand.

Regina looked at Anthony. He sighed. "Regina thinks I hit a trigger."

"What is that?"

"It's usually trauma buried in the psyche," Regina said. "You may be aware of it or not."

Kaley shook her head. "I can't think of anything like that." Knives flashed in her mind, but that couldn't be it. Anthony wouldn't have used a knife on her. But he had said he was going to remove her clothing.

"Don't stress over it." Regina smiled. "It will come to you when you least expect it."

"Is that a good thing or a bad thing?" Kaley didn't like the idea she couldn't remember.

"Neither. Just go with it when the memories surface and call someone." With that, Regina left the room.

"Need anything?" Jordan asked.

"Kaley?" Anthony asked.

"Ask Noah to make me some hot tea, please. He knows how I like it."

"You got it." Jordan left the room.

"Hot tea?"

"It will get me warm and help me settle down. I'm sorry I ruined our scene." The night had started off so promising. She wanted to figure out what happened.

"There's nothing to be sorry about." He kissed her forehead. "Do I need to worry that Noah knows how you like your tea?"

"No. I get cold in the club sometimes, and I'll make some hot tea. Noah jokes it's the only way I can get warm."

Anthony nodded. "Are you getting warm now?"

"Between you and the blankets, yes. The tea will help my nerves." She let her head rest on his shoulder. "I can't believe I safeworded."

"I'm glad you did."

"Why?"

"Something obviously scared you. We do need to talk about it, but I'm not sure tonight is a good time to do it."

Kaley thought about his words. "I want to talk about it. I want to see if we can figure out what made me call my safe word."

Jordan came into the room, cradling a mug in one hand and two bottles of water in the other. "Here you go," he said, setting everything down on the small table. "I'll be outside if you need me."

Anthony propped her up in the bed and handed her the mug. "Be careful. That is really hot."

She grinned as she took the mug and cradled it between her palms. It felt so good. The heat seeped into her veins. She blew on the tea, took a tentative sip, and sighed. "Nothing like a good tea to calm the nerves."

They were both silent as she drank her tea. Her mind kept replaying their scene in the garden, but nothing they had done would have caused her to call her safe word. Yes, it was new to her to be blindfolded and tied up outside, but Anthony was there.

If there was one thing she'd learned it was that he was very protective. Anthony would never have done anything to intentionally hurt her or expose her in any way. "Did someone stumble onto us?" That was the only thing that came to mind.

"No. Drink your tea and quit thinking so hard."

"I can't help it." She drank more of the tea. "Enough." She leaned over Anthony and set the mug on the table. "I remember lying on the mattress, and you put the blindfold on me."

"That's right. You told me it was okay."

"It was. It is. Then you restrained me." She remembered the feeling of his skin against hers. How the restraints made her feel helpless yet powerful at the same time. The power came from knowing Anthony's rapid breathing was because of her.

Then he mentioned how he forgot to take her clothes off before he tied her up and how he'd have to find a way to get them off. "You asked me if I was attached to my clothing and said you were going to cut them off."

Anthony nodded.

Kaley's breathing quickened. "I couldn't see, and…" Oh shit. "Scissors," she whispered, glancing at Anthony's face.

His features tightened. "Yes, I slipped the scissors between your skin and your bra strap, intending to cut it." His voice was like warm caramel.

"I thought…" She shivered. "I couldn't see." Kaley shook her head. She hadn't expected this. It was so long ago, well, okay, several years ago, but she'd dealt with it. Hadn't she? Apparently not.

"What is it, sweetheart?"

"I thought it was a knife." Even now, she could feel the cold steel on her skin, but she couldn't tell the difference between it and what had happened to her years ago. Well, damn. Without thinking she rubbed below her breasts.

Anthony's hands covered hers. "You rub there a lot."

"Oh?" She didn't realize that. "Nervous habit." But so much more. She wasn't ready to talk about this yet. Anthony loved knives. He was into knife play. While he didn't seem bothered that she wasn't, could this eventually hurt their relationship?

"Don't lie to me, sweetheart. Rubbing below your breasts is a lot more than a nervous habit." He brushed a kiss over her temple. "Let's leave this until later. But know this, I would never use a knife on you without us having a discussion about it. It's a hard limit. Not even to cut something away. I would always use scissors."

"Thank you." She relaxed into his hold. "I'm fine." Anthony didn't say anything, and Kaley wondered if she'd ruined their relationship.

Chapter 16

Anthony pulled up to Kaley's apartment building on Friday, surprised to see her waiting outside for him. He slid out of his vehicle. Maybe, if she wasn't too tired, they could go out to dinner. If she was, they could order pizza.

"Hi, sweetheart." He leaned down to kiss her cheek, but she moved away. He frowned.

"We need to talk." Kaley turned and walked into the building. He followed, his curiosity in tow. Once they were inside her apartment, she turned to him, hands on hips.

"You need to stop."

"Stop what?" He wasn't sure what she was talking about. "I won't stop bringing you food."

"Not your responsibility, but we can come back to that. I'm talking about the way you've been treating me like spun glass since last Saturday night."

Damn, he was hoping she hadn't noticed. After her trigger last week, he'd backed off, keeping things light.

"I'm not some sad, weepy woman."

"You're not." She hadn't cried at all last week, and that bothered him too. Emotions were meant to be expressed not held inside.

"Then why are you treating me like one?"

"I didn't mean to. Let's sit down." He gestured to her sofa. Kaley blew out a breath and took a seat. Anthony followed. He'd talked with Max and Jordan on Monday to understand more about triggers.

While neither had experienced them, they had seen them. They told him to give Kaley time to process what happened and not to push. So, he hadn't, but apparently, he'd taken not pushing to a level she didn't like. How did he fix this? Be honest.

"You scared me Saturday night." Showing his vulnerability to Kaley might help her understand.

"I didn't mean to."

"I know." He took her hand. "I'm worried I'll hit another trigger."

"You won't."

"You can't promise that."

She frowned. "So, you're not going to even kiss me because of this?"

"Yes…No…" He ran his hand through his hair, making it spike. "I don't want to hurt you."

"I know you don't." Her gaze softened as she stared at him. "Anthony, I can only apologize for my over-the-top reaction Saturday night."

"You know why you had it, don't you?"

Kaley nodded. "I'm not ready to discuss it, not yet. But that doesn't mean I don't want to try again."

"I understand." He did, but he wasn't over his own fear. "I want to take things slow."

"We have been." She entwined her fingers with his. "I don't mind taking kink slow, but our relationship… I want to keep progressing there."

"You've thought about this."

"All week." She leaned over. "I want you."

He barely prevented his jaw from dropping open. "I want you too." He'd told himself he'd be honest, and he was. He'd wanted her for weeks now.

"Then let's go to bed." She stood up, still holding his hand.

"What about dinner?"

"Later."

Thank goodness Gran was able to be alone all night. Anthony allowed Kaley to pull him to his feet, and he followed her into her bedroom. He'd seen it before since he made sure her apartment was safe, but tonight, it felt different. The brightly colored comforter was pulled back to reveal burgundy sheets. There was a small lamp lit beside the bed.

"Are you sure you're ready for this step?"

"You worry too much." She dropped his hand, grasped his cheeks, and kissed him.

It wasn't the tentative kiss of an unsure woman; it was one of power and need. Anthony let his worries float away. His arms encircled her waist, pulling her to him as he returned the kiss. When they broke apart, they were both breathing heavily.

He rested his forehead against hers. "I'm still a Dom in the bedroom."

"Of course." She grinned.

"Witch." He playfully nipped at her skin. "Undress and get on that bed of yours."

Her eyes gleamed with playfulness as she began undressing. Anthony's mouth watered as she revealed her creamy skin.

He captured her hand when he noticed she was trembling. "We don't have to do this."

"I want to."

"But you're trembling."

"With excitement."

"Oh." He pulled her close. "You've done this before, right?"

Her laughter was music to his ears. "I'm not a virgin, if that's what you're asking." Her warm fingers touched his cheek. "It's because it's you. Anthony. The man who showed me what kink is about, who brings me dinner, and who takes care of his grandmother when she's injured." Kaley tilted her head. "The man who works with underprivileged kids to teach them art, to allow them to get away for an afternoon from whatever situation they're in and be a kid."

"I'm no saint." He brushed a kiss over her lips.

"Not always. You are the man who makes my skin tingle, causes my body to heat, and makes me feel things I've never felt."

Anthony closed his eyes at her description. He didn't feel worthy of her words, but tonight, with her here in his arms, he'd won the biggest prize of his life. Dipping his head, he took her lips in a hard kiss before breaking it off.

"On the bed, my beauty." He forced himself to let her go and watched as she sashayed over and climbed on the bed. Temptress. Kicking off his shoes, he stripped quickly, keeping his gaze on her.

Kaley squirmed on the bed as he stalked toward her. "Hands over your head and spread your legs." She complied. "I won't restrain you tonight, but I will…soon." He moved to the end of the bed and knelt between her legs. "So beautiful."

Anthony ran his palms over the top of her feet, up her legs, to her thighs. "Safe words apply. Okay?"

"Yes, Sir."

His gaze captured hers. "No Sir tonight. We're just Anthony and Kaley, but I want you to feel safe."

"I do."

He lowered his head and licked her slit. Her moan sent a shaft of pleasure directly to his dick. This was for her. He would pleasure her all night long. Settling between her thighs, he licked her again and toyed with her clit.

"Oh, Anthony." Her voice was soft.

He lifted his head. A flush covered her body, her eyes were barely open, and her fingers curled into her palms. This was going to be fun.

* * * *

Kaley fought to keep her arms above her head as Anthony licked and teased her. He played with her clit, then moved to her pussy. Damn, the man had a talented mouth. She was getting wetter by the second, and it usually took her longer than this to warm up.

It confirmed she'd been with the wrong men. Anthony wasn't her past and definitely worth the wait.

Her pussy muscles tightened when he inserted two fingers into her. Tingles spread from her groin throughout her body.

"More," she whispered, trying to catch her breath.

"There will be so much more," he answered.

His tongue toyed with her clit, and he slipped three fingers into her. She bucked against his touch. *Oh lord.* Every nerve ending in her came alive. He pumped his fingers in and out of her as he toyed with her clit.

Her body was primed and ready. "Anthony," she whispered. Her breathing increased, and her toes began to tingle.

"Yes, Kaley."

"I'm so close."

"Then let go." He lowered his head.

His fingers curled inside her pussy, hitting that hidden spot, and Kaley cried out, seeing stars behind her eyelids. She was so close it wouldn't take much to throw her over. Her body trembled with her climax. When she started coming down, she opened her eyes. Anthony lay with his head on her thigh, gazing up at her with a satisfied grin on his face.

"I like those little cries you make when you come." He shifted and crawled up her body. His hair-roughened chest brushed against her erect nipples, causing delicious sensations to flow from her nipples to her clit.

He didn't miss her reaction and grinned. "I'll play with those later." His lips captured hers. She could taste herself on him, and she didn't mind. His cock was hard against her stomach, and she wiggled.

"Want you," she whispered when he broke the kiss.

His blue eyes deepened. "Your wish is my command, my lady." He shifted, rolled a condom on, and his cock brushed her entrance.

Kaley let out a sigh as he slid his dick into her. So hard, yet so warm. Unable to help herself, she lowered her arms and curved them around his back.

"You're touching me," he whispered.

"I have to." Her fingers played over the muscles in his back. "I need to hold on."

He chuckled. "Then hold on to me, my lady." Anthony shifted.

Her eyes closed as he withdrew and sank back into her pussy. This was wonderful, magical even. She was connected to Anthony on a level she couldn't explain. Maybe that's why she'd avoided him for so long.

"I must not be doing a good job if you're thinking so hard." He slid out and back in.

"You feel so good."

"That's my line." He kissed her as he began to move a little faster. Her breathing hitched in her throat.

"So powerful," she whispered when he released her lips.

His fingers traced her cheek before moving slowly over her collar bone, between her breasts, and over her belly. He tapped her clit with his finger.

"Damn." Tingles swept through her body from her toes to her head. "You're a menace."

"I'm yours."

She closed her eyes. How she wished she could be his. For now, she assured herself. He set a punishing pace while his finger toyed with her clit.

"I'm not going to last long." Her fingers dug into his back.

"Let go for me. Let me feel your pleasure."

Before she could blink, he pinched her clit, and Kaley cried out as her orgasm swept over her. Twice in one night, that was new. But he didn't slack off. He kept his pace and another climax built.

"I want to see your pleasure this time," she whispered, opening her eyes.

Anthony kissed her and surged into her. He threw his head back and moaned as her pussy pulsed around his cock. For time eternal, they lay there, hearts beating at the same fantastic rate, her core tightening further to keep him inside her until the last possible moment. Keeping his weight off of her, Anthony rolled to his side, taking her with him. Keeping them intimately connected.

"So beautiful," he whispered, pushing her hair away from her face.

"I could say that about you." Kaley kissed him softly. She wanted to lie in his arms forever. Her heart skipped a beat as she remembered how different their lives were. How impossible a lifetime with Anthony seemed to her. Thrusting those thoughts from her mind, she rested her head on his shoulder and closed her eyes. Tomorrow was soon enough to think. Right now, she just wanted to feel.

She could so easily fall in love with Anthony was her last thought, and it didn't scare her as much as it should have.

Chapter 17

Anthony smiled as Kaley walked behind the bar, wearing her new purple and white wristband. He'd talked with her about it. He didn't want other Doms hitting on her, and it gave her another layer of safety. She was doing the early shift tonight—eight until ten. Last night had been wonderful. Holding her all night and waking her with caresses that led to more caused his grin to widen.

While he'd like to have spent the day in bed with her, she had dogs to groom. So instead, he went home and worked on her painting. It was coming along nicely. She'd asked to see it, but he told her not until he was finished. He didn't tell her she'd become his new muse, and he had several paintings in various stages since she came into his life.

"You look like the cat that swallowed the canary," Dane said, walking up to him.

"I'm just happy," Anthony replied.

"Does it have anything to do with the pretty sub behind the bar sporting a new wristband?"

Anthony laughed. "Maybe." Dane was a friend, and he'd taken a chance on hanging Anthony's art in his gallery. Something that had worked out for both of them.

"I'm glad to see you happy." Dane clapped him on the shoulder. "When can I expect new pieces for the studio?"

"Soon. I've got a couple that are almost done." None of them would be Kaley. Nope, he'd decided those were his.

"Perfect."

Anthony looked up as John approached. "I can wait until you're done," John said.

"We are." Dane walked away.

"What do you need, John?"

"I was wondering if you'd demo some knife play with my sub. She's been wanting to try, and I'm not ready to go that deep yet."

"I'll need to check with my sub first." He wasn't going to leave Kaley out of this conversation. They hadn't talked much about his knife play. "Be right back." Anthony sauntered over to the bar and waited until Kaley was free before he signaled her.

"What can I get you, Sir?" Her brown eyes sparkled with mischief.

"A minute of your time." Anthony leaned close to her. "A Dom is asking me to demo knife play on his sub."

He didn't miss the slight shiver that went through her body even though she tried to cover it up.

"What does this have to do with me?"

"We're in a relationship, and you're my sub. I won't do anything with another sub without asking you first."

Surprised flashed over her features. "Oh. It's just a demo, nothing more?"

"No, nothing more." Was she jealous? She was the only one he wanted.

"I don't see why not."

"Thank you." He brushed a soft kiss over her lips before he walked across the room to John. "All is good. What time do you want to do this?"

"Ten-thirty, if that works. Master Max is setting up an area."

Anthony nodded. "I need to get my kit out of my truck, but that's fine."

"Thank you." John walked away, and Anthony turned to gaze at Kaley.

She moved behind the bar with grace, but her movements were a little jerkier now, and her ready smile seemed stilted. He wondered why. Would doing knife play with another sub upset her? He hoped not, but they really hadn't talked about it. Kaley didn't like knives, and the reaction she'd had to the scissors showed him how much. He rubbed his forehead.

He'd have Damon keep an eye on her during the demo. No way did he want to trigger her again.

* * * *

Kaley tried to control her nerves. Anthony considered them in a relationship, yet he was going to do knife play. Ice chased up her spine as she rubbed below her breasts. Would she ever get over her fear of knives?

Her therapist thought she would, but she could barely deal with the sharp knives she used in the kitchen. Was she doing Anthony a disservice by being with him when she couldn't handle his kink?

Not that he'd said anything. It really hadn't come up in conversation, and it was a hard limit on her questionnaire.

"You're thinking very hard." An amused male voice penetrated her thoughts.

"Hey, Noah." She'd tuned everything out.

"You okay?" He held his hand up, and she nodded, then he placed it on her forearm.

"I am." She liked Noah and trusted him. "I have a question for you."

"Go for it."

Kaley glanced around; the bar was pretty empty. "How would it make you feel as a Dom if your sub couldn't handle some of your kink?"

Noah frowned. "Is someone trying to make you do something against your hard limits?"

"No." Kaley captured him by the upper arm before he could stalk away to find Anthony or even Max. "It's a general question."

"It's more than that." He stared at her. "No Dom worth his salt would be upset. They would talk with you about it, and if you couldn't handle it, they would let it go."

"But what if it's something they love and you don't."

"Same answer, Kaley. While they may do the kink with someone else with your permission, it doesn't mean they care about you any less."

Kaley let out a breath, her muscles easing. "Thanks, Noah." She went on her toes and kissed his cheek. "That helped."

"Why are you kissing him?" Anthony asked.

Kaley turned her head. "I was just asking his advice on something. No need to get your hackles up, Sir."

Noah laughed. "Kaley, Doms will always get their hackles up when they see their sub, their woman, with another man. But in this case, you have nothing to worry about, Anthony." He stepped back. "Go play with your Dom."

Noah walked away, and Kaley glanced at Anthony. He was staring at her. "It was nothing. A question I needed answered."

"You can ask me anything; you know that, don't you?"

"Yes, Sir, but this was something I needed an unbiased opinion on." She stepped close to him. "You and I are involved, and you might be a little prejudiced."

Anthony smiled and captured her by the waist, pulling her to him. "Damn right, I'm biased when it comes to you. Let's walk around a bit."

"When is your demo?"

"In about thirty minutes."

Kaley nodded. She had time to build up her wall and not let anything that happened penetrate.

* * * *

Anthony led her to a sofa right in front of the play area. Tessa was there with Damon. "We'll keep an eye on her," Damon said when she sat down.

"If you have any questions, ask them." Anthony brushed a soft kiss over her lips. "Later tonight, I'm going to take you to the edge in bed."

Heat flared through her body at his words, and she ducked her head as he walked away. Tessa patted her hand. "Anthony's a good guy."

"I know." Kaley was conflicted. She wanted to watch Anthony with his knives, but another part of her wanted to run as fast as she could.

"Payne is so good," Damon said.

"Pain?" Had Damon said what she thought.

"Stop it, Sir." Tessa swatted Damon's arm before turning back to her. "Silly nickname. It's a play on his name."

"I don't get it." Kaley stared at them.

"P-a-y-n-e is his last name," Damon clarified.

"Oh." Her gut clenched. In none of their play did Anthony seem like a sadist, but what did she know. Her attention was caught by Anthony walking up on the stage, and he laid out his knives. When had he brought those in? Did he leave them in the club all the time? No, she remembered seeing them at his home.

"Good evening, everyone. John has asked me to work with his sub tonight. Give us a few minutes, and we'll get started." Anthony's voice was strong and sure.

Kaley kept her gaze on him as he talked with John and his sub. John nodded, and the sub smiled before John led her to the bondage chair sitting at the front of the stage. Kaley shifted as John restrained his sub.

John stepped back, and Anthony brought out a blindfold. "I use a blindfold so the sub is unaware of what I'm doing. Not all subs need one, but in most cases, they do."

Anthony placed the blindfold on the sub and stepped back. While the music in the club had been turned down, it was the only thing she could hear as everyone waited for Anthony to make his move.

Anthony touched the sub's head, and she jumped. The audience let out a sigh. "He loves to mind fuck with subs when he scenes," Damon commented.

Kaley didn't react to Damon's words. She was too busy watching Anthony. When he picked up a small knife, her tummy tumbled over, and she stopped breathing. He ran the flat part of the knife down the sub's arm.

But all Kaley saw was the light reflecting off the blade. Her vision grew dark. She couldn't do this. "Excuse me." She slipped out of her seat and nearly ran out of the club, never looking back.

In the ladies room, Kaley took big gulps of air. Oh, God. What was she going to do?

"Kaley?" A warm hand touched her shoulder, and she jumped.

"Sorry." Tessa stood next to her.

"I…" Tears filled her eyes.

Tessa opened her arms and enfolded Kaley in her arms. "It's okay." Tessa led Kaley over to the bench and sat down with her. "Does Anthony know you're afraid of knives?"

"How…" Kaley lifted her head.

"It's written all over your face."

"He does. It's a hard limit." Kaley rubbed below her breasts as if to sooth a sore spot. "I thought I could watch, but I couldn't."

"It's okay." Tessa soothed. "One thing Damon was right about is that Anthony's knife play is a mind fuck."

"But he could so easily cut the sub. Cause a real injury."

"He's good at what he does." Tessa rubbed her back. "You need to discuss this with him."

"I don't know how." She didn't. Kaley wanted to be with Anthony, but she wasn't sure she could ever accept his need for knife play.

"Just talk with him. He'll understand."

But would he? Kaley worried Anthony wouldn't understand at all. Knives were a part of his kink makeup.

"I may be crossing line here, but have you thought about talking to a therapist about it?" Tessa asked.

"I have."

"I mean a kink friendly therapist."

Kaley stared at her. "There's such a thing?"

"Yep. Just a second." Tessa went to her locker, pulled out her cell phone, and texted someone. Within a few minutes, her phone pinged. "Here. She's kink friendly." Tessa handed Kaley her phone.

The therapist's name jumped out at her. She'd been seeing this therapist for years. Who knew. "Thanks." She texted herself the information so Tessa wouldn't know any different. Her next appointment was going to be interesting.

"You're welcome. Don't feel pressured about going. I just want every one of us subs to be happy."

Kaley gave a half-smile. "I am happy with Anthony."

"Good. Then keep those lines of communication open." Tessa put her phone back in her locker. "Shall we go back in."

"Yes." Kaley stood and ran her hands over her body. "Thanks, Tessa."

"Anytime."

Chapter 18

Anthony put his knives in their case and turned to look for Kaley. He didn't see her. Frowning, he carried his knives to his locker and locked them up. When he came out of the men's room, he caught sight of Kaley and Tessa standing in the reception area.

"There you are." He smiled at them.

"Done so soon?" Kaley asked.

"Yes. Are you okay?" He stared at her. Something was off, but he couldn't put his finger on it.

"I'll see you in the club," Tessa said, leaving the two alone.

"Yes…no….oh heck, I don't know." Kaley shook her head.

He frowned. "Let's go sit down and talk." Anthony took her arm.

"Yes, let's, but first…" Kaley threw her arms around his neck and kissed him.

Anthony automatically encircled her waist and kissed her back. Holding her this close, he could feel the slight trembling of her body. He broke the kiss and stared down at her. "You're not okay. You're trembling."

"I know." She snuggled against his chest.

Anthony sensed something wasn't right. He kept Kaley close to his side as they walked back into club. Luckily, there was an open sofa in the quiet area. He pulled her onto his lap when he sat.

"Want to tell me what's going on?"

"Not really." She laid her head on his chest.

"I can't fix it if you don't talk about it." And fix it he would, no matter what it was.

"What makes you think you can fix it?"

"I'm a Dom."

Her laughter caused several heads to turn. "Men."

His mood lightened with her laughter. "I'm glad I could make you relax."

"I'm always relaxed with you." She ran her finger over his chest.

"You left the demo early."

"You noticed?"

"I observe everything."

"Your attention should have been on the sub."

"It was, but that doesn't mean I don't pay attention to my audience." He tightened his arm around her shoulders. "Did it bother you to see me with another sub?"

"No." She wiggled against him, and damn if his cock didn't react. But he pushed his need away. He wanted to understand what was going on with her.

"Then what?"

She let out a sigh. "Can we just sit here, like this, please?"

He wanted to say no, but she snuggled closer to him, and he couldn't. "All right, but we will discuss this." Anthony rested his cheek against the top of her head. He needed to know why she'd walked away. He didn't want secrets between them. Ever.

* * * *

Anthony looked at his phone. Kaley canceled on him, again. It was Friday night, and all week she'd had excuses for why he shouldn't bring her dinner. He was tempted to ignore her excuse for tonight, but something held him back.

In his studio, he stared at the painting of her. She'd sat for him last Sunday, but her spark was missing. There was something most definitely going on with her. If only he could get her to talk to him. Cleaning up, he slipped on his club clothes and headed for Wicked Sanctuary. Maybe one of the more experienced Doms could help him understand what had happened with Kaley.

Anthony spied Damon when he entered the club. He'd been sitting with Kaley during last Saturday's demo, so maybe he'd have some insight. "Evening, Damon."

"Hey, Payne."

Anthony hid a wince. He didn't mind the use of his last name, but some days, it cut him deep. He was so careful not to cause the subs pain. "Do you have some time to chat?"

Damon's features went from playful to serious in a second. "Sure." Damon turned, and Anthony followed him into the quiet area of the club, if there was such a thing. At least here, the music was muted, and they would be able to hear each other.

"What's up?" Damon asked after he sat down.

Anthony put his elbows on his knees and leaned forward. "You were sitting with Kaley during my demo last Saturday."

"I was."

"Did she act funny to you?"

Damon crossed his arms over his chest. "What do you mean by *funny*?"

"I know she left the demo not long after it started. Did she say anything?"

"Shouldn't you talk to her?"

Anthony sighed. "I've tried. She's put me off with excuses all week. I don't know what to do."

Damon rubbed his chin. "I was watching her out of the corner of my eye since she's new to the club. All I could tell was that she looked a little uncomfortable. Kaley plays her cards close to her chest."

"Yeah." Anthony had noticed that too. Usually, subs were very expressive but not Kaley, unless she was completely relaxed or working with her animals, then the joy on her face was there for everyone to see.

"Don't let her retreat," Damon said.

"I don't want to push." He was worried if he pushed too hard, she'd avoid him even more.

"I'm not saying push her. Keep yourself in her life. Text her, call her, heck, video chat with her. Let her know you're there for her. Show her you want the two of you to be together."

"I'll think about it."

"I'd also ask her why knife play bothers her so much."

Anthony tilted his head. "How do you know that?"

"Besides her walking away from the scene? The entire time, she was rubbing a spot below her breasts, like something hurt."

"I've noticed that. She told me it was a nervous habit."

"It could be. She's been in the club less than six months, but you're the first person she's played with or even gotten close to."

"What about Noah? He was her trainer."

"She and Noah have an easygoing relationship. He was teaching her the aspects of kink and how the club worked. But there was no spark. You, on the other hand, make her light up."

"Thanks." Anthony had a lot to think about.

"Work it out in your head and then go after her. I believe in my heart she's your keeper." Damon stood and left Anthony alone. Yes, he had some more thinking to do.

Chapter 19

Kaley pulled into the parking lot of Sweet & Savory at one on Friday afternoon. She'd rescheduled her afternoon clients so she could have a chat with Dani. She needed to talk to someone.

Walking into the brightly lit café, Kaley relaxed. She needed the afternoon off. She'd been working far too hard this week, mainly to keep her mind off of Anthony. Not that it worked; he was never far from her thoughts.

"Kaley," Dani called.

She turned and saw her friend sitting at a table in the corner. "Thanks for meeting me." Kaley took the empty seat across from Dani.

"Not a problem."

Kaley's stomach rumbled. "I guess I'd better get something to eat." Her budget could handle having lunch out. "Be right back." She walked to the counter, ordered a bowl of soup and two beef empanadas, plus some iced tea.

Back at the table with her tea, she placed the number at the end. "I should have asked if you want something."

"Lara's bringing mine in a few." Dani waved her hand. "I eat here so often she knows what I like." Dani studied Kaley for a minute. "What did you want to talk about?"

Kaley swallowed and took a sip of her tea as her mouth dried out. "Ummm, a little bit ago, you did a demo with Anthony with his knives." A shiver ran through her body.

"I did."

"Can you tell me about it?" Kaley had talked with her therapist, who also happened to be the kink therapist Tessa had given her. Her therapist suggested talking with someone about knife play, someone she trusted to tell her the truth. She also reminded Kaley about what happened to her was years ago, and while traumatic, Kaley had made great strides and not to let something like this cause a backslide.

"What do you want to know?"

"Everything."

Dani laughed. "Tall order." Lara brought Dani's and Kaley's orders at the same time, then left.

"Were you nervous?" Kaley asked.

"A bit. Mainly because it's something I've never tried before." She took a bite of her sandwich.

Kaley nodded as she took a bit of her empanada. "I didn't see much of it. Did..." Kaley swallowed. "Did it hurt?"

Dani's eyes widened. "Absolutely not." She put her sandwich down and reached across the table and rested her hand on the back of Kaley's. "It's all a mind fuck."

"People have said that, but I don't quite understand."

"Let's see if I can explain." Dani withdrew her hand. "It was something new to me, too, but I'd been wanting to try. I've watched Anthony with other demos."

Kaley nodded.

"Some consider it mind manipulation, and it can be. In the wrong hands, knife play can create harm. You won't see that at Wicked Sanctuary."

"But Anthony does it."

"In a minor aspect. He uses his voice and tone to create a world with his knives, but one thing I know for certain. He has never drawn blood or intentionally hurt someone."

"His knives look sharp."

"Oh, they are. If you've ever seen him work with them, you'll notice how he makes sure the tip and sharp edges are never against a sub's skin. It's all about the sensation of the cold metal against one's skin, not about drawing blood."

"But accidents can happen." Kaley rubbed below her breasts.

"They can, but not with Anthony. He might act like he's done something wrong. A few months ago, during another demo, a Dom poured chocolate syrup over the sub's arm after Anthony ran the dull edge of his knife across the skin."

Kaley hand fluttered to her chest. "What happened?"

"The sub let out a cry. Anthony stepped back as the Dom grabbed her before she panicked."

"But she could have panicked and caused Anthony to hurt her."

Dani shook her head. "I'd heard Anthony and the Dom discuss it before the scene, so Anthony was prepared. Trust me, if Anthony ever hurt someone, he'd destroy his knives."

"How do you know that?" Kaley still couldn't think about knife play with Anthony, but this helped her understand how important it was to him.

"He's always improving his skill. Do you know he still goes and works with the Master he learned from?"

"He does?" When did he find time for that? Probably while she was working.

"Yes, before I did the demo with him, Anthony insisted on chatting with Gabriel and me about it. Max is careful about what he allows in the club, and one of the prohibitions is no blood."

Kaley nodded. While the information helped her, it didn't make her fear diminish. "Thank you, Dani. This has helped."

"If knife play is a hard limit, Anthony won't violate it."

"I know he won't." That was one thing she was sure of. The question now was could she watch him doing knife play in the club? And could he feel the same way about her that she felt about him if she could never take this step with him?

Chapter 20

Anthony was frustrated and maybe a little bit angry. Kaley had been behind the bar all night. It was now after midnight. He'd been sitting at the bar off and on, but she'd kept busy and only stopped to ask what he wanted to drink and to refill his sparkling water.

She was ignoring him, and he didn't like it not one bit. She hadn't even let him drive her tonight, insisting she'd get a ride. He found out that Noah had driven her. Jealousy reared its ugly head for a moment before he realized Noah had given several of the subs a ride that night.

He kept his gaze on Kaley as Max walked up to her and pulled her aside. He could see Max wasn't happy. Anthony was about to go over to the pair when Kaley nodded, and Evan took her by the arm.

Oh, hell, no. Anthony was on his feet crossing over to the pair before Max stepped in front of him.

"Excuse me, Max."

"No." Max put his hands on Anthony's shoulders. "You need to let her be."

"It isn't like you to interfere," Anthony said, his gaze on Kaley and Evan.

"I normally wouldn't, but Kaley asked me to find her a ride home tonight. Evan is leaving early and giving her a ride."

"I can take her home." He drew his hand through his hair.

"I know you can, but when I suggested it— Let's just say Kaley vetoed the idea."

"What the hell?" Anthony shook his head.

"Did you two have an argument?"

"Not that I'm aware of. She's been acting squirrely since my demo." No matter what he did, Kaley was a step ahead of him. Why wouldn't she talk to him?

"Have you talked with her?"

"I've tried." Anthony took a step back. "I've called her, left messages, I don't know what's going on."

Max stared at him. "Give her some time."

"How much time, Max? She's shutting me out."

"I can't answer that. Did you do anything that might have set her off?"

"I know you're trying to be helpful, but we've only done light play outside the club. I tried to talk to her after the demo, but she didn't want to talk about it."

"What happened at the demo?"

"She left after the first couple of minutes. I couldn't stop the demo to go after her."

"Of course not, but you said you tried to talk to her."

"I did. She cuddled in my lap, but refused to talk about what was happening."

"Who was she sitting with?"

"Tessa and Damon. I've talked with Damon; he said Kaley seemed uncomfortable and kept rubbing her abdomen."

Max glanced around the club. "Let's go have a talk with Tessa." The two men crossed the club to where Tessa sat with Sierra and Crystal. "Tessa, Anthony and I need a moment please."

"Of course." Tessa stood and the trio walked over to a set of chairs.

"Did you chat with Kaley after the demo last Saturday?" Max asked after they sat down.

"I did." Her spine stiffened.

Dread filled Anthony's gut at Tessa's defensiveness.

"What did she say?" Max asked.

Tessa shook her head. "I'm sorry. I won't divulge a conversation between two subs done in confidence. I'm sorry, Max." She looked at Anthony. "What's going on?"

"Kaley's avoiding me," Anthony said. He trusted the sub network. The subs protected each other, but they also helped each other.

"Not surprised. All I will say is that she's scared."

"That doesn't help." Max crossed his arms over his chest.

"Again, Max, I won't reveal anyone's secrets. You know we subs have a code."

Max nodded but didn't look happy.

"If there's anything you can do to help Kaley, I'd appreciate it." Anthony didn't know what else to say. The subs were a tightknit group, just as the Doms were. They would protect their own.

"I'll check in with the others and see if one of us can talk to her. We'll do our best, but Anthony, all I can say is give her some time. She needs to work through her feelings."

"Thanks, Tessa." Anthony stood and walked away. Well, while Tessa hadn't been able to say much, a couple of things stuck out: Kaley was scared, and she was fighting her feelings. Now all he had to do was figure out how to get her to let him back in.

Chapter 21

Anthony hauled the last painting into the gallery a little over a week later. "You've been busy," Dane commented.

"You asked me for more pieces."

"I did and expected one or two, not five." Dane began to unwrap them.

"I'm going to go wander around the gallery while you do your thing." Anthony didn't want to stay while Dane looked at his work. Sleep had eluded him, so he painted instead. He found a quiet corner and leaned against the wall.

Kaley still hadn't contacted him. He texted her every day, letting her know he was there for her, but she was the one who had to take the first step. As much as he wanted to push, he wasn't going to.

"I love Anthony's work." A female voice floated over the partial wall.

"Yes." Another answered.

"He's so handsome, but I think he has a dark side."

Anthony stayed quiet. He wanted to hear what these women had to say.

"What do you mean?"

"Look at how he's drawn the women. Subservient to men. His work is harsh toward women as role models."

"True. But there's something elemental in his painting. Maybe he's working out his pain with his mother or something."

The other woman laughed. "Oh, you don't know. He doesn't know who his parents are. He was adopted by the Pierces."

The women's voice dropped. "Really? Are you sure that's not gossip."

"It's not. I heard Olivia talking one day, and she mentioned Anthony wasn't her biological child."

"Interesting. That might be why he's chosen to do fetish art."

The voices drifted away, and Anthony didn't move. The women were wrong. The observers' remarks were typical of the myths surrounding the lifestyle. Submissives had to be insightful, self-aware individuals. It took a strong person to give over most or all control to another person.

Was he living a pipe dream about his art? Dane had taken a chance on him, and Anthony didn't want there to be any blowback on Dane or his gallery. Would he ever be worthy to people?

Interesting how his adoptive mother actually talked about him not being her biological child. Neither of his adoptive parents had told him he was adopted until he was eighteen and refused to do what they wanted. That had been one hell of a fight.

"There you are," Dane said, walking up to him. "I love the new work, and since you're here, I'll give you this."

Dane handed him an envelope. "What's this?" Anthony turned the envelope over and opened the flap.

"Your cut from the paintings I've sold."

Anthony slid the check out and froze. "There has to be some mistake." He could only stare at the check.

"No mistake. I made sure it was a cashier's check so there wouldn't be any issues with the bank."

"But…" He shook his head.

"Trust me. People love your art."

"Not everyone." He thought about the two women he'd overheard talking.

"Who cares about them? There are enough who enjoy your work. Trust me, I'm not going to have any trouble selling the new ones."

"Thanks, Dane." Anthony pushed the envelope into his pocket and left. It was a little bittersweet that he'd found success, but the woman he wanted to share it with wasn't talking to him. After a quick stop at the bank to deposit the check, Anthony stopped and picked up two bouquets of flowers.

One for his grandmother and one for Kaley. He checked his watch. Kaley was due to groom Nugget today, and he wanted to be there when she did. Climbing into his vehicle, he headed for home.

* * * *

"You spoil me," his grandmother said when he handed her the flowers. He laid the second bouquet by the front door.

"No, I don't." He kissed her cheek and watched her as she crossed the kitchen to get a vase. Her ankle had healed, and she was getting around on her own. She had been for a couple of weeks, and Anthony was happy to see her thriving and independent again.

"You do. You took care of me when I hurt my ankle, and you're constantly doing things around the house and the cottage to keep them in good repair."

"It's the least I can do."

Clara looked at him as she sat down. "What do you mean?"

"You took me in when my adoptive parents threw me out."

She threw her hands up in the air. "Those two are idiots. You are my grandson, and I wasn't about to see you homeless."

"Don't think I didn't notice how you lost friends over the years because I was here. I'm not worthy of your love."

"Anthony Payne Pierce you stop this right now."

The use of his full name got his attention, especially since he'd dropped the Pierce name years ago.

"You are more than worthy. I didn't manhandle you into seeing the therapist for you to think like that. Don't let these"—she waved her hands again—"ignorant people make you think you are anything but a wonderful human being."

He fought against grinning at her using the word *manhandle*. All she'd done was insist he get into her car and told him it was time to get his head on right. "But, Gran," he started.

Clara shook her head and reached over and took his hand. "I watched my son and daughter-in-law the day they brought you home. They were so happy, and you were always a perfect little boy."

Anthony barked out a laugh. "I was far from perfect."

"Scrapes all kids get into. But you grew up into a young man who knew what he wanted from life and who wasn't going to have his wings cut."

"They couldn't accept me as I was."

"It was more than that. They had unreasonable expectations, and when you decided to do things your way, they thought you'd cave to their wishes."

"I might have if it hadn't been for you. You gave me a place to live, a chance to explore my art."

"Because I saw it was a part of you. I love you, Anthony. No strings. No expectations. You are my grandson, period."

Anthony blinked, then he stood and went over to his grandmother, knelt next to her chair and enfolded her in a hug. "I love you, Gran."

"Good. Now what is going on with you and Kaley?"

"What?" The change of topics threw him as he stood up and retook his seat.

"I'm not blind. She hasn't been around much lately, and you're not taking her out or anything. You've been spending way too much time in your studio working."

"Do you miss anything?"

"Nope. Is that what all this unworthiness is about?"

He shook his head. He admired Kaley so much. She'd struggled all her life to make her way while he had a life of privilege. Hell, even with being kicked out at eighteen, his grandmother made sure he survived.

Kaley never had that. She had to do everything on her own. Anthony sat back in his chair. He could make things easier on her. But would she accept his help? Hell, he couldn't even get her to talk to him.

"It'll be fine, Gran. We've just hit a rough patch." An idea formed in his head. There was knock at the door. "I'll get it."

"Charm her."

Anthony was grinning when he left the kitchen. It might take some doing, but he was going to find a way to get over the wall she'd erected.

* * * *

Kaley stood with Nugget in her arms. She'd bathed and groomed him in her van today, hoping to avoid Anthony. Clara's injury had healed, but she was still moving a little slow, and Kaley didn't feel right just walking in. She waited. The door opened, and she gasped.

"Anthony." Well, so much for avoiding him.

"Hi, Kaley, come on in." He held the door wide and gestured for her to enter.

She swept past him, noting he smelled like turpentine. Had he been painting? Stupid question. Of course he'd been painting; that was his job. His passion. Along with knife play. A small shiver flashed through her body. Nugget wiggled, and she set him down, and he ran for the kitchen.

"How are you?" Anthony asked, shutting the door.

"Okay. How about you?" Great, now they were stuck in polite conversation mode, but she didn't know how else to respond.

"Tired." His voice was soft. "Can we talk?"

"I…" She didn't have a client for a couple of hours. "I have some time."

"Good." He gestured for her to proceed him, then put his hand on her arm. "Are you okay being alone with me?"

Kaley blinked. "Yes." She wasn't lying. She still hadn't made a decision about how to move forward with him, and it gnawed at her insides. She didn't want to hurt Anthony any more than she wanted to be hurt.

"All right." He gave her a half-grin. "Gran, Kaley and I are going to my place for a little bit."

"Nugget looks so good. Thank you, Kaley."

"You're more than welcome." Anthony gestured to the front table. "Those are for you, so don't forget them on the way out."

Kaley glanced at the front table to see a bouquet of flowers. Her heart warmed as he guided her to the back door and then over the path to his cottage. Once inside, he gestured for her to sit.

"Would you like something to drink?"

"No, thank you." Damn, she felt like a fraud, sitting here trying to making polite conversation. Her stomach twisted, and she started to rub below her breasts but stopped herself.

Anthony grabbed a straight-back chair, spun it around, and straddled it. "I don't know where to start."

His words were soft, and Kaley took a breath. "I needed time to think."

"About what?"

"Us."

He stiffened, and Kaley wanted to curse for saying the single word, because she'd thought about so much more than just the two of them together.

Anthony gripped the chair back, then released it along with a slow, pent-up breath. God, she hated that she was putting him through this.

"Can we start with why you've been avoiding me?"

She spread her hand in front of her. "You kind of swept into my life."

"If I pressured you in any way, I didn't mean to."

"You didn't." How could she explain this to him? The last thing she wanted to do was hurt Anthony, but she needed him to understand. "This is about me, not you."

"That sounds familiar." His shoulders slumped.

"I have some issues I need to work through." Wasn't that the truth. She'd been seeing her therapist again, but it had only been a couple of sessions.

"What can I do to help you?"

His voice held concern, as did his eyes. The ice wall around Kaley's heart started to melt, and as much as she wanted to keep it there, where Anthony was concerned, it was a losing proposition.

"I have things I need to work through myself, and I need space to do that. I'm okay with us having dinner together, just not every night."

"I can live with that. What about us being together in bed?"

Kaley rubbed her hands on her thighs. "I'd like that." When he opened his mouth, she held up her hand. "When the time is right."

"And at the club?" He could leave club play out if she wanted, as long as he could be with her.

"I'll still be there on Saturday nights, but by myself. I'm sorry, Anthony. I don't want to hurt you, but that's all I can handle right now." Even now, the tug to be with him almost overwhelmed her. If she gave in, she'd never deal with her past, her issues. And eventually, her fears would slice their relationship to shreds, leaving both of them in pieces.

He nodded. It was better than nothing. "I can live with that. Will you come and sit for me on Sundays again?"

"Every other week."

He rubbed his forehead. "You're limiting our time together, why?"

Kaley rubbed below her breasts. "Yes. I have some private issues to figure out."

"Don't we all," he muttered. He extended his hand, and she placed hers in his. "I want to be with you is all."

"We will be. Just a little slower than before." Maybe she'd rushed their relationship the first time. The knots in her stomach began to untangle.

He nodded. "Then I'll see you Saturday." Anthony squeezed her hand.

"Yes."

"If you ever need a ride, ask me. I'm here for you, Kaley. Always. Will you spend time with me after your shift?"

Her lips turned up. "I will."

His features lightened, and Kaley's muscles relaxed. Baby steps. She could do this.

"Thank you." He squeezed her hand again before releasing it. "I guess I should let you get back to work."

She nodded and stood. Anthony followed suit. He grabbed the flowers as they walked out the door and to her van. Once there, he captured her hand and turned her to him. "See you Saturday night." He leaned over and brushed a light kiss over her lips before placing the bouquet in her arms.

Before she could react, he straightened, released her hand, and was walking away. Kaley climbed into her van and placed the flowers on the passenger seat but didn't leave. She put her fingers to her tingling lips.

She glanced over at the flowers. White and red roses. He must have spent a fortune on them. Kaley shook her head. She wanted to be with Anthony. She missed him the past few weeks; it was her own fault. But until she dealt with her issues, she had to be strong. It was going to be a long few days until Saturday.

Chapter 22

Kaley all but ran into Wicked Sanctuary, changed, and then headed into the club to get behind the bar. Thank goodness she'd gotten a ride with one of the other subs.

"Not like you to be late," Noah commented.

"An appointment ran over." She blew a strand of hair back.

Noah stared at her before nodding and walking off. Kaley took a deep breath and got to work, not that there was much going on. Two Doms sat at one end of the bar chatting, and that was it. The rest of the bar was empty.

Actually, the club wasn't as full as she was used to seeing, and she wondered what that was about when Jordan wandered up to the bar. "Evening, Kaley."

"Master Jordan. The club seems empty tonight."

"Yes. There's a festival a couple of towns over. It impacted the club due to traffic and whatnot."

"Oh." She hadn't even thought about it.

"We'll probably close early if it doesn't pick up."

"How early?"

"We're talking two instead of four." He smiled. "Not too early."

Kaley glanced over as Anthony walked up. "Jordan, Kaley."

Her heart sped up. Anthony was bare chested tonight. His tats were on display; that was new. Her mouth watered as she took him in. The man was sculpted and, combined with a pair of low riding cotton pants, downright kissable.

The club doors opened with a bang, and Logan Wolfe walked in still dressed in his police uniform. He made a beeline for Jordan.

"I know I'm not dressed right," Logan said as he approached Jordan. "I'm on duty. I came to tell you there's a major accident on the main road to the club. We're doing one way traffic control."

"Anyone hurt?" Jordan asked.

"Life flight is on the way. It's not a pretty sight. But you may want to tell everyone. It'll take them all a lot longer to get home tonight. They'll close down the road for the life flight, and even after that, it's going to be one way traffic control until tomorrow morning."

Jordan nodded. "Thanks for letting me know."

Logan gave them a wave and left.

"Well, that changes the plans for tonight. Kaley, will you cut the music please."

"Sure." Kaley turned the music off, and Jordan moved onto one of the stages.

"Attention," he yelled. "I was just informed there is a major accident on the main road, and it will be closed for a little bit, then open with one way traffic. The club will be closing in fifteen minutes so everyone can get home."

"Good thing it's a light night," Anthony said.

"Yes. I hope those involved are okay." Kaley began putting things away and wiping down the bar.

"May I drive you home?"

"Yes. I'd appreciate that." The second Jordan finished his announcement, the sub she'd caught a ride with ran out of the club. "I'll be done here in a minute, then I can change."

"I'll be waiting."

His 'I'll be waiting' warmed her heart. The conversation with her therapist today had hit home. They talked not only about her fears but how Anthony made her feel, and why she was flipping between fighting against being with him and wanting to be with him. There was no easy fix. It was all up to her. She finished cleaning up and then changed. Anthony was lounging next to the front door when she walked out.

"All ready."

"Be careful," Jordan said.

"I will. I have precious cargo." Anthony slipped his arm around her waist and guided her outside to his vehicle. "I'm glad I brought the SUV tonight."

"You have more than one vehicle?"

"The SUV and a car. Sometimes it's not practical to drive the SUV." He held open the door and helped her up into the SUV.

"I'll turn the heat on once the engine warms up," he said.

"I'm fine."

"I saw that shiver. Our summer is over, and temps are starting to fall." He pulled out onto the main road.

"True, but I'm not cold. I hope we don't have a bad snow season this year." She gazed out the window.

"Last year was unusual. Did it affect your business?"

"Yes. I couldn't drive to see clients." She laughed. "Pleasant Valley is just in the right spot to get caught in some of those darn snow storm. I was snowed in for two days before the plows got to my neighborhood, and even then, it was too icy to drive."

Anthony frowned. "I don't like to think of you driving in those conditions."

"I do my best not to. If it's a little dusting, I'm okay, but I really do hate the ice." She noticed the red taillights ahead of them as Anthony slowed down. When he stopped, he turned off the engine. Kaley glanced at the line of waiting vehicles. "I wish there was a way around this."

"One of the issues with Max having his club out here," he said. "The road dead ends at the campground."

"Yes, it's never been a problem before?"

"Not that I've seen. I'm not sure how long we're going to be here." He opened his door. "Be right back." Kaley saw him talk to a couple drivers in front of them and then walk back. But instead of climbing in, he went to the back of the SUV.

The tailgate opened and then closed. When Anthony opened his door, his arms were full. "Good thing I'm prepared." He tossed several blankets onto the center console and then placed several bags on the dashboard.

He closed his door and made sure the locks were engaged. "I know it's early, but the temps are predicted to drop to forty tonight. We have blankets to keep warm, water in the back seat, and some snacks if we need them."

"You're the perfect boy scout."

"I might be prepared, but trust me, there is nothing boy scouty about me." He wiggled his eyebrows, and Kaley burst out laughing. If she had to be stuck with someone, Anthony was a great choice.

"You talked to the other drivers; what did they say?"

"The car in front of us is Dane and Regina. They arrived shortly before us, but the driver of the other car said he'd already been here for thirty minutes." Anthony pulled out his phone. "I'm going to check the traffic app and see what it says."

Kaley waited silently until he let out a sigh. "Not good news."

"According to this." He wiggled his phone. "It's going to be hours. They've reopened the road but are doing one way traffic control four cars at a time."

"Well, it can't be helped."

"You always have a sunny attitude."

"Not always." She released her seatbelt and shifted in her seat.

"Well, what shall we do? I don't have a deck of cards or we could play strip poker."

Kaley laughed. "Strip poker in a car?"

"Okay, maybe go fish, but since that isn't possible, and I don't want to drain our phone batteries. What would you like to talk about?"

She swallowed. Her therapist had told her that she needed to explain to Anthony about her fear of knives and why. Was this a good time? Her gut clenched.

"I didn't think it was that hard of a question."

"Sorry."

"Sweetheart, you don't need to be sorry. Just talk to me."

"About what?"

"What are your dreams for your business?"

Kaley barely hid her shock at the question.

"You weren't expecting that, were you?" He tapped her nose. "I know you have plans."

"I do." She shifted. It didn't matter how comfortable a vehicle was, once stopped, everything began to ache from sitting, and they hadn't been there more than ten minutes.

"Tell me your plans. Your dreams. I want to know."

"Only if you tell me yours."

"Deal, but you're going first."

"I want to establish a dog grooming shop but not just that. I want to be able to have people bring their dogs in, and I want to keep the mobile grooming business as well."

"But if people can bring you their dogs, why do you need the mobile unit?" He tilted his head.

"Not everyone is mobile or wants to drive."

"Like my gran."

"Yes, so this way I can accommodate those who want to take their animals in with those who prefer home services."

"That's a nice plan. How is it coming along?"

Kaley relaxed against the seat. "Good. It's still going to take a couple of years, but I've got a steady income."

"Sounds like a solid plan. Can I ask about where you live? Have you thought about moving to a better neighborhood?"

Her lips twitched. "I wondered when you'd bring that up." He held his hands up as if to fend her off. "It's been better since the front door lock was fixed, and all the lights are now working."

"It doesn't mean I like it."

"Anthony."

He placed his hand on hers. "I only want you to be safe."

She sighed. "I know. Now tell me your plan and dreams." He didn't remove his hand from hers, and she didn't move either. She liked his warmth on her skin.

"Well, my dream of being an artist has worked out better than I could have imagined since Dane put my work in his gallery."

"You deserve it."

He inclined his head. "There are times I wonder if I do or not. I've found that not everyone likes my work."

"Human nature is fickle."

"True. But I do have a big dream." He turned her hand over, and their fingers entwined. "I want you in my life."

Kaley sucked in a breath.

"It might be too soon, but I wanted you to know that. These past few weeks—the distance between us— have been hell."

"I'm sorry." Her fingers tightened around his. "I should—"

The sound of his phone ringing cut her words off.

"Hold the thought." He picked up his cell from where he'd set it on the dash. "Hello. Yes. Okay, thanks, Max." He turned to her. "Max invited us to come back to the club and make use of one of the private rooms tonight."

Kaley stiffened.

"Not to play, but to sleep. It looks like the road is going to be tied up for a while since we haven't moved an inch."

"What about Dane and Regina?"

Before Anthony could answer Dane was at the driver's side. Anthony turned the vehicle on and lowered the window. "Max just called me," Dane said.

"Me too. Are you heading back?"

"Yes. No sense in spending the night in the car. You two?"

Anthony looked at Kaley.

"Us too." She gave Anthony's fingers another squeeze. This was the right thing to do.

"Great. I'll pull out and make a U-turn—that will give you more room." Dane walked back to his vehicle.

Within a few minutes, they were on their way back to the club, and Kaley's stomach knotted with the confession she still needed to make.

Chapter 23

"I appreciate you allowing us to stay here," Anthony said to Max as they walked into the club with Dane and Regina. The lighting was minimal.

"No problem. Most people didn't make it here due to the accident, those who did have found places to hang out or are willing to just wait in their cars. I'd invite you to the house, but Jordan and Crystal claimed one room already, Lara and Colby the other one. Noah and Bennett are in rooms one and three."

"It's fine," Kaley spoke up. "We appreciate your offer."

Anthony tightened his arm around her waist. She'd been quiet on the drive back, but held his hand, and when he put his arm around her, she didn't shy away from him. Maybe the accident had done him a favor.

"We prepared rooms two and four for you. There are extra blankets if you need them. Also, Sierra insisted on having some food and drinks put in each room. If you need anything, give me a call. You can bet Sierra will want all of you to come to breakfast tomorrow." With a wave, Max was off.

"Which room would you like?" Dane asked.

"It doesn't matter," Anthony said. It didn't. Just being with Kaley was enough.

"Let's take four," Regina said with a grin.

"Night." Dane led Regina to the room and shut the door behind them.

Anthony glanced down at Kaley. "We can stay out here until you're ready to go to bed." He didn't want her to feel pressured.

She glanced around the club and shivered. "I'm okay. Let's go into our room."

He liked how she said 'our room'. He guided her to the door, threw it open, and they walked in.

"Oh my." Kaley's quiet words held him still.

The room was decorated in red and black. There was an X frame in one corner, a spanking bench in another. Several cabinets and the bed…steel frame with red drapes hanging from the top.

"Not what I was expecting," Anthony said, closing the door behind them.

"Do you think Dane and Regina knew?"

"I have no idea." He guided her farther into the room. Any other time he might have been excited by the room, but tonight was about Kaley, not sex and not play.

Two small tables sat near the door, one had water, juice, and two bottles of wine and glasses, and the other food. There was a covered platter and snack food. Kaley's stomach grumbled

"You didn't eat before you came tonight," Anthony commented. At least there were two chairs from the club in the room. He wondered if Max put them in the room before they got here.

"An appointment ran late."

"Let's see what we have here." Anthony released her and pulled the cover off the platter. "Looks like stuff from Lara's café."

Kaley come up beside him. "Lara was catering tonight. I was going to grab some food after I got off shift." She lifted one of the bagel dogs and bit into it. "Still warm. I'm starving."

"Give me a minute." He pulled the table out and then arranged the chairs around it. "Your dinner awaits you, my lady." He bowed and held out a chair for her.

"Thank you, my knight."

Her words went right to his heart. He wanted to be her knight in shining armor. Not that she needed one, but it stroked his ego.

He sat, and they dug into the food. Bagel dogs, chicken empanadas, and a couple of deli sandwiches. All in all, not a bad dinner. "Dessert?" he asked gesturing toward the plate of brownies and cookies.

"I'm full." Kaley rubbed her belly. "What time is it?"

Anthony pulled out his phone. "A little after ten." He tidied up the table and moved it back with the other one. "Water or juice?"

"Water, please."

He brought her a bottle and then sat back down. "Before Max's call, you were going to tell me something. What was it?"

Her eyes widened as if she was surprised he remembered. Her mouth opened, and there was a knock at the door. Damn all these interruptions. Anthony opened the door.

"Hi," Sierra said. "I hope I'm not interrupting anything."

"Sierra," Kaley said, standing up. "Thank you for the food."

"It was nothing." Sierra held out the bundle in her hands. "I thought you might like to change and not sleep in your clothes. I'm not sure of the fit. They'll probably be too big."

"That's very kind of you." Anthony took the bundle from her.

"Have a good night." Sierra walked out the door.

Anthony closed the door and dumped the bundle on the bed. "Let's see. Some sweats, t-shirts, and sweatshirts. Packages of underwear, toothbrushes and toothpaste." He placed everything out on the bed. "A comb and brush as well."

"That's so sweet of Sierra."

"It is. I wonder how they have packages of underwear?"

Kaley giggled, and he stared at her. "Sub joke."

"Explain, please."

"Right after I joined, there was a small party at Lara's café with all the subs in attendance. It was a mini celebration of Sierra's upcoming marriage." She giggled again. "Anyway, the joke was to bring a present for the couple, but it had to be an intimate present. This was the result." She gestured to the underwear.

"The subs gave her underwear?" He shook his head.

"Yep, these are the normal ones. There were crotchless, thongs, edible ones. It was really quite funny."

"Thank goodness we didn't get the others." Anthony bit his lip so as not to blurt out that he'd love to eat the edibles off of Kaley. "How would you like to do this? I can step outside while you change."

Kaley shook her head. "We've been naked in front of each other before. It's fine. Besides I'm starting to feel chilled. I'm more than ready to get beneath the covers." She blushed the cutest pink—another reason he was so taken with her.

Anthony grabbed the package of men's underwear and a pair of sweats and moved across the room. He turned his back to give her some privacy.

While she was right that they'd been naked in front of each other, it had been a few weeks ago. He quickly undressed and put on the new clothes. The boxers and sweats fit nicely. He folded his clothes and put them on top of the cabinet.

"I'm going to turn around."

"Okay."

He turned and couldn't hold back grin. Kaley had to roll up the sweat pants, and thankfully, they had a drawstring because, otherwise, they would have fallen off.

"Stop grinning." She pushed up the sleeves of the sweatshirt. "I feel like a little kid, and I'm not a small woman."

"Compared to Max you are." He walked over to her and framed her face. "At least this way you can be comfortable."

She shrugged. "I guess."

"I'll put your things with mine." He took her folded clothes and put them with his before turning back to her. "How do you want to handle this?" Anthony gestured to the bed.

It was a large king bed, but he didn't want her to worry about something happening she didn't want. He could take the two chairs and rest.

Kaley walked over to him. "I think we can share a bed." She caressed his cheek.

"Lights on or off?"

"Off."

"Get in bed first." Once Kaley was in bed, he switched off the lights. While the light had been subtle, now the room was filled with dim light from the exit sign over the door, and one emergency light in the corner. Anthony waited a minute.

His eyes had adjusted, though not perfectly, but he could see the outline of the bed and made his way over and sat down.

"Better get under the covers. I doubt there's a lot of heat in the club."

Anthony chuckled. "Usually too many bodies to worry about it." He slipped under the covers. He could see Kaley on her side facing him.

"Now what?" she whispered.

He settled on his side, facing her. "How about we finish our conversation before Max's phone call interrupted."

She sighed. "About what you said."

"Yes. I'm not going to be shy about wanting you in my life, Kaley." He reached out and cupped her cheek. "I want to be with you, and we can work out any issues we have as long as we communicate."

"Oh, Anthony." She placed her hand over his where it lay on her cheek.

"These last few weeks have been hard." Beyond hard. Anthony wanted her to understand where he was coming from. Not to shame her or anything, but to let her know he could share his feelings.

"They have for me too." She shifted closer to him. "I'm sorry. I needed some time."

"You said that, but why did you need the time?"

"Because I was afraid."

The words hung in the darkness around them. "Of me?"

"Not you. Never you." She let her hand drop from his. "This isn't something I like to talk about, but it's been pointed out to me that I should talk about it."

Anthony shifted, wondering who had pointed that out to her. He slipped his hand from her cheek to her waist, but kept his arm above the covers. "Whenever you're ready."

"That may be never."

He tightened his arm around her to let her know he was here for her, but otherwise stayed silent.

"It happened when I was twenty-two." Her voice was soft. "I was working two jobs, trying to get my feet under me so I could start my mobile business."

"You told me you worked as a dog groomer in a salon."

"I did. I didn't tell you that I had a second job." She shifted again. "I usually worked as a groomer from seven until four, then I went to my second job."

"Which was?"

"I worked at the emergency vet clinic from five until eleven at night as a receptionist."

"That couldn't have been easy on you." He drew her closer and was pleased when she laid her head on his shoulder.

"No, but I was able to help people who needed help with their animals." She blew out a breath. "I was leaving work one night, a couple days before payday, so I decided to walk home."

He stiffened.

"I know." Her hand moved to his chest and rested there. "At the time, I didn't think anything about it."

"Where were you living?"

"Where I am now. Anyway, I was almost home when a guy stepped in front of me. I kind of ignored him and stepped around him. Then he caught me by the arm and spun me around."

Her body shook.

"It's okay, sweetheart." He gathered her close.

"I know what you're thinking; he didn't sexually assault me."

Anthony blew out a breath.

"He wanted money. As I said, it was before payday. I think I had a whole ten dollars in my pocket. That didn't make him happy. He started waving a knife at me." Her voice trembled. "I found out later he was high on drugs. He stabbed me."

"Kaley." His arm tightened around her.

"I was lucky. It missed any vital organs."

"You ran out on my demo because of that." Now things were becoming clearer in his mind. Including why she reacted the way she did in the garden. The scissors reminded her of a knife.

"It's more than that." She tilted her head and their gazes met. "My father used to wave knives around and threaten us kids when he was drunk."

Anthony didn't know what to say. No wonder she was afraid.

"After your demo, Tessa followed me into the bathroom, and we chatted, and I also talked to Regina. I thought I was moving past it all, but what happened in the garden caused a flashback. That told me I hadn't moved past it. Plus, that night, watching you…"

Anthony nodded. "The scene in the club." Damn. He'd made things worse and caused her to relive some of the worst moments of her life. He felt like a world-class heel. "I'm so sorry, Kaley."

"Please don't be. I need to get past this, and you've helped kickstart that. I'm in therapy, again."

"You don't sound happy about it." Therapy was probably the best thing for her, and if they survived this, he'd have to discuss maybe going together. Perhaps he could use some therapy himself. Guilt was currently eating a hole in his stomach.

"I thought I'd dealt with it, but wham, out of nowhere, the fear rolled over me, and I…" She bit her lower lip. "I don't know if I can ever accept knife play."

"You're worried about that?" Astonishment hit him in the gut.

"You love knife play, and it wouldn't be right of me to ask you to give it up. You worked hard to be good at it."

"Kaley." He shifted and brushed his lips over her nose. "I knew knife play was a hard limit for you, and that's fine. Maybe at one point I thought about talking to you about trying it, but I can live without us doing knife play."

Her eyes widened. "But I can't even watch you do it."

"That doesn't matter either." All this time, she was worried about him. "Yes, I enjoy knife play, but it isn't all about the knives. I don't know how much you've seen me do."

"Very little." She shivered.

"It's more about getting inside someone's head. I don't use knives to cut people or make them bleed. It's all about making them think I'm going to cut them, but it's all in their mind. I do that by using words and sensations."

"I think I understand." She yawned.

"We've talked enough for tonight. Close your eyes and rest."

"You're not mad?" Her voice had a tinge of fear to it.

"Of course not." He shifted until he could get his free arm around her. "You're afraid; that's understandable. We can get through it together. I'd like to help us both get through this."

She started to speak, but he put his hand over her mouth. She'd stopped shivering, but the tension in her body was easy to feel.

"No more tonight. Relax. Close your eyes. I'll be right here."

"Yes, Sir," she mumbled against his hand and closed her eyes.

Anthony laid awake a long time after Kaley relaxed in his embrace and slept. Knives were the issue, not him. Well, maybe there was a little bit of him wound up in it. Tomorrow, they'd discuss how they were going to proceed.

Chapter 24

Kaley woke to the smell of coffee. She opened her eyes to see Anthony sitting next to her holding out a mug. "Coffee?" she muttered.

"Just for you."

She sat up and took the mug from him. "What time is it?"

"Almost nine." He sipped from his own mug.

Nodding, then taking a sip of her coffee, she moaned. "This is so good."

"Lara brought it to us. She said breakfast is at nine-thirty."

The night before came flooding back: the accident that blocked the road, coming back to the club, talking to Anthony about knives. Her hand trembled.

"Hey." He took the mug from her before she spilled her coffee and set it aside with his. "What's bothering you?"

"I…" She swallowed. "I told you about my fear."

"You did. And I'm humbled you shared your secret with me. Now we can deal with it." He caressed her cheek. "Will you show me where you were stabbed?"

Kaley lifted the sweatshirt she was wearing to just below her breasts and rubbed the spot between them. There was a faint scar. It was barely noticeable, but she knew it was there.

"May I?" Anthony held his hand up.

She nodded and held her breath as his touch replaced hers. His touch was delicate and tender. "I'm so sorry you were hurt this way." His voice was low.

"Thank you. It wasn't your fault."

"No, it wasn't, but I still feel bad that it happened. Did they ever catch the guy?" He removed his hand and gave her back her coffee mug.

"Yes." She was grateful for the warmth of the mug in her hand. "In some ways, I was lucky. The guy had a rap sheet, and he knew he was in trouble. He confessed and was sentenced to ten years in jail."

"Good."

Kaley stared at him.

"I like the idea that he's locked up."

"I get it. I'm just glad I didn't have to go to court and testify. For a long time, I could barely stand being alone."

"How did you cope?"

"I got therapy." She was matter of fact about what she did. "My therapist helped a lot. She told me it could have happened to anyone, and after a while, I realized she was right."

A knock sounded on the door. Anthony got up and crossed the room. Kaley watched his tight ass as he walked. Her breath hitched in her throat.

"Hey, Max," he said after he opened the door.

"Here's your freshly laundered clothing. Come up to the house for breakfast in twenty minutes."

"Thanks." He took the bundle of clothes from Max and shut the door.

Kaley was already on her feet. "They washed our clothes?"

"Yes and no. When I woke, you were sleeping, so I took them up to the house and asked if I could use the washer and dryer. I'd just put them in the dryer when Lara told me coffee was ready and when breakfast was." He sat them on the bed. "Finish your coffee. Then we can go to the club bathrooms and clean up."

She nodded. A quick brush of her teeth and hair would make her feel better, not to mention being in her own clothes. When she finished dressing, she stood there and stared at herself in one of the mirrors. She'd told Anthony what happened.

In some ways, it made her feel free—a burden had lifted off her shoulders. She wanted to let go of her fear, but she wasn't sure she ever could completely.

* * * *

"Your family kidnapped you?" Kaley almost choked on her food at Lara's words.

"Yep. The idiots," Lara said.

Kaley could only stare at her.

"Your family is as bad as mine," Crystal said. "My father tried to take me back to that darn backwater town I grew up in and make sure I understood it was God's will."

Jordan's hands covered Crystal's. "They can't hurt you anymore," he said softly.

"I know." Their fingers entwined.

Kaley sat there, realizing there was trauma in the others' lives as well, and they seemed at peace with it.

"I guess I'm lucky. My family only kicked me out for wanting to be a nurse," Regina said.

"That makes no sense." The words burst from Kaley's mouth.

"It doesn't. But their loss is my gain." Dane placed a kiss on Regina's cheek.

"My ex-boyfriend took me to a horror campout even though he knew I'd hate it." Sierra turned to Max. "The only good thing was that it brought me to Max."

"It did. You looked like a drowned kitten that night, but you took my breath away." Max grinned at Sierra.

"I didn't realize…" She swallowed. Face your fear. The words her therapist spoke during their last session echoed in her ears. "I was stabbed a few years ago in a random robbery."

All eyes turned in her direction. Anthony shifted in his seat, his hand on her thigh. Kaley covered his hand with hers and gave it a squeeze.

Everyone started talking at once. Kaley sat there, absorbing all the love. That's what it was. Voices of concern, but also kindness and understanding. This is what she'd been missing all these years. People who cared…and understood.

"Is that why…" Regina trailed off.

"It's okay, Regina. Yes, it's why I triggered; I'm afraid of knives."

Max nodded. "Makes sense now."

Kaley glanced at Anthony. His eyes were shining with… She didn't know what. He looked proud of her.

Conversation returned to more mundane subjects, and they finished breakfast, then made their way to the car. When they were on their way, Anthony reached over and took her hand in his. "That was brave of you to talk about your fear at breakfast."

"Once I told you, it was a relief. It was easy to tell them." She shook her head. "I didn't realize how much trauma they'd been through."

"Most of us have trauma in our lives."

"I never really thought about it. What's your trauma?" Silence filled the vehicle, and Kaley turned to look at Anthony. His expression was thoughtful. "I'm sorry. I shouldn't have asked."

"It's okay." He lifted her hand to his lips and kissed her fingers. "I'm adopted."

"Oh." While it didn't sound traumatic to her, maybe it had been for him. "How old were you?"

"I was a little over a year old."

"You must have been so scared." She could only imagine a one-year-old losing the only family he knew and being given to strangers.

"I really don't remember."

"Have you ever thought about finding your birth parents?" She'd read stories about adoptive kids looking for their birth parents.

"No." His chest rose and fell with his deep breath. "From what I understand, my birth parents gave me my name and then gave me up."

Her heart hurt for him. "Maybe they couldn't take care of you?" She was trying to be logical but couldn't quite understand why someone would give up their child. But then again, it happened every day in this world.

"Maybe. Anyway. I was adopted by the Pierces."

"Pierce? Wait a second; I thought your last name was Payne."

"Payne is my birth parents' last name."

Kaley tilted her head. "But you didn't take the Pierce last name?"

"I did. But I dropped it."

"Dropped it?"

"Yes, long story, but when I was eighteen, I took back my birth parents' last name."

"As long as you're happy." She grinned. "Besides you're special to me not matter what your name is."

His lips tilted up. "You might not think so in a minute. My adoptive parents are Olivia and Albert Pierce."

"What?" She knew those names, only because she was on the internet. They were cream of the crop society people in Pleasant Valley. She and Anthony really were from different sides of the track.

"I know. Shocking isn't it that they have a son who's a fetish artist."

She heard the bitterness in his voice. "You are a great artist." Kaley wasn't about to let him put himself down. "You have such talent. I'm so glad Dane is displaying your work so people can see it. It's bringing the lifestyle more attention. Good attention."

He stopped the car at a red light and turned to her. "You mean that, don't you?"

"Of course." She leaned closer to him. "I'm so proud of what you've accomplished."

Their lips met in a soft kiss until a horn honking interrupted them.

They broke apart with a laugh.

Anthony reluctantly dropped her off at her apartment, but only after Kaley insisted. She had things she needed to do to get ready for work on Monday. But before he left, Anthony told her he'd be back to take her to dinner.

She agreed. It looked like their relationship was back on, but in the back of her mind, she still wondered how long it would last. His family had money. Heck, Anthony had money. She'd seen how much his paintings sold for.

Even if he only got a fraction of that money, he was still a heck of lot richer than she was.

How long before Anthony resented her lack of resources?

Chapter 25

Kaley finished up her paperwork for the business and closed her laptop. The last week, she and Anthony had seen each other every night. He left her with scorching kisses that made her want to tear his clothes off.

Even last night in the club, they'd stuck together. While they hadn't played, they had gotten a little hot and heavy with each other. Nothing that people in the club hadn't seen before, but Noah commented they needed to get a room.

Today there was a sub meeting at Lara's café, and Kaley wanted to be there. She really enjoyed these meetings. It was a safe place for the subs to talk, and she finally felt like she could contribute to the conversation.

It was a nice day for the beginning of fall and Kaley decided to walk. She didn't mind the long walk; it gave her time to think and get some exercise at the same time. She arrived at the café to see the subs gathered around a table.

Kaley checked her phone. She wasn't late; it wasn't even two yet. All eyes turned to her when she walked in. "Ah. Hi."

Sierra broke away from the group and walked up to her. "Hey, Kaley." Sierra took one of her hands. "I'm so glad you could come today. All of us here talked, and we want to help you."

"Help me?" Kaley was confused.

Regina stepped forward. "Yes." She waved at the other women who stepped aside and revealed the table.

Kaley stopped breathing. Knives. They were scattered around the table.

"I knew this was a bad idea," Crystal said, coming up to Kaley's side. "It's okay. You don't even have to go near them."

"It's not that I don't appreciate…" A shudder racked her body.

"Too soon," Tessa said. "Ladies, let's put them away."

"I'm sorry." Sierra's voice was wobbly.

"Sierra." Kaley took her hand. Sierra looked ready to cry. "I know you're trying to help me, but this isn't something that's easy to get over."

"Sometimes I'm like a bull in a china shop. I think of something to help and can't see the other side of the coin." Sierra sniffled.

"None of that." Tessa grinned, pulling Kaley toward the now empty table. "Let's talk about how we're going to figure out what our men are hiding behind that big tarp in the club."

* * * *

Anthony stood, watching Kaley on Friday night at the gallery. Dane had arranged for this event, and he'd asked Kaley to go with him. She'd been unsure, at first, but he convinced her. She was across the room chatting with Regina. While he'd been with her every night in the past few weeks, he was still amazed by her. He would bring her dinner; they would talk, make out, and sometimes he'd go home, and other nights he wouldn't.

Life was looking up. He was finished with her paintings. Yes, multiple. While he had her sit for the one, his mind kept her image in the forefront all the time. Now, they were done.

"You look like you're ready to eat her up," Dane commented, coming up to him.

"I am."

"Good." Dane clasped him on the shoulder. "Thanks for doing this tonight. I know these kinds of events are not your favorite thing."

"Usually not." But tonight he didn't mind with Kaley at his side. She looked delicious in the black cocktail dress. Her legs seemed to go on forever.

"Well, I appreciate it." Dane glanced at the door. "Oh boy."

"What?" Anthony turned to see his adoptive parents walking into the gallery. What were they doing here?

Albert saw him and guided Oliva toward him. Both were dressed to the nines, their strides confident. Anthony wanted to run, but he couldn't. He was an adult. He could deal with them. Yes, he avoided them like the plague. Mainly because he didn't want to be reminded that they thought him worthless because he hadn't followed the path they wanted.

"Anthony."

"Albert." His father winced when Anthony used his name. "What are you doing here?"

"Excuse me," Dane said and walked away.

"We came to see your work, honey," Olivia said in an overly sweet voice.

"Oh? Really? Neither one of you ever seemed very interested in my art before." Hell, they'd wanted him to give it up all his life.

"We're here." Oliva waved her hand like she was shooing away a fly. "Show us your work."

Anthony was about to refuse when Kaley walked up to them. "Hi, I'm Kaley," she said with a bright smile and extending her hand.

"Albert Pierce and my wife, Olivia." He shook Kaley's hand.

"How nice of you both to come and support Anthony." Kaley curled her hand around his arm. He appreciated her support. "Are you going to show them around?"

Anthony gazed down at Kaley. His irritation at this very unpleasant surprise vanished. She was here with him. She supported him in ways he didn't know he needed. "Yes. You'll join us, right?"

"Wouldn't miss it." He gestured for Albert and Olivia to follow them as he walked over to his first exhibit. It was one of his tamer paintings as the subjects were clothed but no less sensual.

He watched Oliva press her lips together, while Albert's fingers curled into his palms. They definitely weren't here for his work. There was another reason. He wasn't going to allow them to embarrass him.

"Excuse me," Regina said. "Can I steal Kaley for a minute?"

"Of course." Anthony released her but brushed a kiss over her soft lips. "Hurry back."

"I will."

With regret, he watched her walk away with Regina.

"We need to talk. Shall we step outside?" Albert asked.

"Fine." Not that they really had anything to talk out. Once outside, Albert and Olivia took up a position on either side of him, and Anthony was about to ask them what was going on when a flash went off.

"Thank you," the cameraman called out.

While there had been press at the initial premier night of Anthony's work. Dane had told him tonight was more low-key. That could only mean one thing. Anthony turned to Albert.

"So that's what this is all about," he said, trying to hold on to his temper.

"What's the harm in a little family photo?" Albert said, stepping away.

"Your father is thinking of running for town council," Olivia said.

"He's not my father." Anthony stepped back from the pair. "I should have guessed it wasn't my paintings you wanted to see." He was mad at himself for the little bit of hope that had flared in his gut that maybe they'd finally come around. He was a fool. "This is all I've ever been to the two of you, a prop. I'm not doing it anymore."

"Please." Albert hissed out the word. "What you do isn't art. It's porn."

"It's beautiful," Kaley said, walking out of the gallery and to his side. Her eyes were flashing daggers at Albert. "Anthony's art is special. There are few artists that can capture the sensuality he brings to the canvas."

Albert shook his head, while Olivia stuck her nose in the air. "You may think so, young lady. But Anthony's drawings are anything but art."

Kaley stiffened, and Anthony hid a smile. She was defending him and his art.

"Enough." He kept his voice low, but the command was there. "You got what you wanted. It's time for you to leave."

With a huff, they walked away into the night. Anthony looked down at Kaley. "You didn't have to defend me."

"What is their problem anyway?"

"I'll explain later, but for now. I'm glad you're here." She deserved so much more than him. Maybe he should call off their relationship. They'd just gotten back together. He let out a sigh. Why wasn't life easier?

* * * *

Anthony loosened his tie as they walked into his cottage. He walked into the kitchen, intent on pouring himself a whisky, when he stopped short. Kaley was with him, and she didn't do alcohol. She didn't mind if he had a beer or wine, but hard liquor… He shook his head and started a mug of coffee.

"Do you feel like talking about what was going on?" she asked, putting her arms around him as she pressed against his back.

"Do you mean my parents?" He pulled the first cup of coffee from the machine and started another one.

"Yes." Her arms tightened around him. "They were rude."

"I don't know why they bothered." The second mug finished. "Actually, I do know. They wanted a photo op. The perfect little family." The bitterness in his words surprised even him.

"Anthony." Kaley's voice was soft, and her arms tightened when he tried to slip out of her hold.

"It's who they are. They never cared about me." He pried her arms from around him and stalked over to the fridge, pulling out milk and pouring it into her mug.

"They must have cared at some point. They adopted you."

He picked up their mugs and gestured to the family room. If he was going to tell this story, he was going to do it in comfort.

Kaley sat on the sofa as he placed her mug on the table in front of her and took his seat in the overstuffed chair. Anthony cradled the mug in his hands, enjoying the warmth.

"While they adopted me, I don't think they ever loved me."

She opened her mouth and closed it.

"No argument?"

"I can't." She took a small sip of her coffee and set it back down. "You know about my parents."

"We both have seriously messed up families."

"But you have your grandmother. I know she loves you."

A hint of a smile caught his lips. "Gran was the one stabilizing force in my life."

"Why did your parents come tonight if they don't like your art?"

"They hate my art. That's how I found out I was adopted."

"What do you mean?"

"I've always loved drawing, even as a kid. But they wanted me to find a more practical job. Luckily, because of electives in high school, I was able to keep them happy and myself. But when I turned eighteen, I wanted to go to art college."

"That makes sense."

"I had a big fight with them and then Albert blurted out that I wasn't his biological child, so was it any wonder I turned out the way I did." He set his mug down. "When I questioned his words, he told me in no uncertain terms that they adopted me, and I owed them."

Kaley stood and knelt in front of him, her hands on top of his. Her support meant the world to him.

"When I refused to change my mind, they kicked me out."

"What?" Her eyes grew wide.

He nodded. "That first night I slept in my car, the one I'd bought myself by working odd jobs. I had no idea what I was going to do." He sighed. "I was woken the next morning by Gran banging on my window. She told me to drive to her place; she'd be there shortly."

"I can see Clara doing that."

"She's a force to be reckoned with, that's for sure. Anyway, she waltzed into her house thirty minutes later and informed me my clothes and other belongings would be delivered later in the day and to go pick out a bedroom."

Kaley squeezed his fingers. He locked his gaze with hers and saw the sheen of tears in her eyes.

"I wasn't alone. Gran made sure I got my belongings and helped me. We rarely talk about Albert and Olivia, then or now."

"I'm glad she was there for you."

"Me too. I probably wouldn't be the man I am today without her."

"You're a good man. I don't care what anyone says."

He slipped his hand out from underneath hers and touched her cheek. "I think you might be biased."

"Damn right, I am." She leaned into his touch. "But that still doesn't explain tonight."

"I avoid my adoptive parents like the plague. Apparently, they came into the gallery tonight to have some photographer take a picture. Albert is running for the city council."

"Oh."

"It doesn't matter. I'm done with them. I have a new life, and I want it to be with you." He urged her up and onto his lap.

Kaley laid her head on his shoulder. "You are special, Anthony."

"I'm glad you think so." Maybe, just maybe, he was finally starting to believe it.

"I do." She placed a soft kiss on his lips.

Chapter 26

Kaley slid behind the bar with a familiar feeling. It had been two weeks since Anthony's adoptive parents ambushed him at the gallery. Yes, that's how she thought of it. While Anthony said he was over it, Kaley was worried. He'd been spending a lot more time in his studio lately.

He made time to bring her dinner or have her come to his place, though. They spent most nights together, and oh, how glorious those were. Time stood still when she was in Anthony's arms. She never wanted it to start up again.

Last Sunday, Kaley reviewed her finances and was surprised to find she was almost at her goal. She'd been working hard to get to this point, and with winter coming soon, it gave her the cushion she might need.

Anthony sat down, and she brought him a glass of sparkling water.

"Hi, sweetheart." He leaned over and brushed a kiss against her lips.

"Hi, again." He was acting like he hadn't seen her all night, yet they'd driven in together.

"Do you want to scene tonight?"

"I'd love to." She really wanted to play with him some more. Not that they hadn't, but this was different. Anticipation flowed through her veins.

"Good. I'll have Max reserve an area for us."

"What do you have planned?"

"A surprise." He grinned, and Kaley's smile faltered. "Nothing that will be past your limits, I promise."

She nodded as Max walked up. "Evening, Anthony, Kaley." He clapped Anthony on the shoulder. "Kaley, Noah is going to take over. Sierra would like to chat with you."

"Oh." Kaley ran her hands over her boy shorts. "Is everything okay?"

"Yes. She told me she needed to talk with you now."

"Okay." Kaley shrugged. "Be back in a few minutes." She slipped out from behind the bar and walked over to the area where Sierra and the other subs were sitting. "What's up, Sierra?" she asked.

"I didn't want to spring this on you, but I was outnumbered." She gestured to where the other subs were standing. Crystal, Tessa, Regina, Allyson, Rose, Lara, and Dani. "We all want to help you with your fear."

Kaley stiffened. "Sierra…"

Sierra held up her hand. "I know, but this time we did it differently. Nothing scary."

The women standing in front of the table parted. While the table held knives, they were
household knifes. Steak knives, cutting tools, even a butter knife.

"Are you okay?" Crystal asked.

"What is this?" Kaley asked, proud her voice was steady and calm.

"I thought maybe since you told us you were working on your knife phobia, this might help," Sierra said. "These are knives we use in everyday life."

"And these," Tessa waved her hand at the small gathering of items at the other end of the table. "Are non-sharp items that can be used in knife play."

Kaley glanced over and then moved to that side of the table. There was a rubber knife, little claw things with rounded edges, several feathers, a metal spatula, and a metal spackle spreader. She reached out and touched each one.

"Anthony uses these?" She hadn't noticed them when she was in his studio, but she had to admit she never really looked.

"Oh yes," Regina said. "It's really to get inside your head, not about pain or hurting you."

"But I've seen his knives. They all look so sharp." She shivered.

"Of course, his knives are sharp. Dull knives can hurt someone more than a sharp one," Rose said. She lifted her arm. "This small scar was made from a dull knife. I know it sounds funny, but it happens."

Kaley raised her hand to rub the spot below her breasts and then stopped herself. It was a habit, one she intended to break. These items didn't scare her. While she was super careful with kitchen knives, she could pick them up and use them.

Her fear nudged her in the gut, but she was determined to understand what Anthony's kink. She reached for the rubber knife.

* * * *

"Oh fuck no." Anthony took off across the club with Max hot on his heels, quickly catching up to the table the subs stood around. The breath left Anthony's lungs when he saw Kaley holding a knife. A knife! If it activated her fear to where she shut down, he'd never set foot in this club again. "Easy with that, sweetheart," he said to Kaley, reaching for the knife.

"It's okay. It's rubber." She put her finger on the tip, and it wiggled.

He breathed a sigh of relief and dropped his hand until he saw the items on the table. "What's going on?"

"They're helping me get over my fear." She placed the rubber knife back on the table.

"There's no need. It's a hard limit, and I understand it."

Kaley shook her head. "For the first time since the attack, I think I might want to try. Some day."

"You don't have to. I can live without it." He could. He wouldn't do anything to hurt Kaley, mentally or physically. He loved her.

He loved her. The words bounced around in his head. This was why, over the last two weeks when he'd been lost in his work, he needed her close to keep him grounded, knowing she was there for him.

"You look a little shell shocked." She took his hand.

"I think I am." He framed her face with his palms. "You're the best thing that has ever happened to me."

Her cheeks went pink. "I have to say, being with you has been different."

"It has for me too. You don't use me as a way to gain favor with my father."

Kaley stiffened in his hold. "What the hell are you talking about?"

The anger in her voice surprised him. "My parents have always used me as a prop. Others have tried to use me to get to my father. You don't do that. You see me."

"Of course, I see you." Kaley took a step back, causing him to release her face. "Anthony, you're more than worthy. You're the kindest, gentlest, funniest, sexiest, and most loving man I've ever known."

Her words were like a balm over his heart. "I love you."

"I love you too, and have almost from the beginning. You aren't getting rid of me that easily."

A cheer went up from the group around them.

He grinned, then pulled her into his arms and claimed her lips. When he broke the kiss, he stared down at her. "Be right back."

"Where is he going?" Max asked.

Anthony sprinted to his car and then back in, carrying his painting. It was time. He looked at one of the stages. Perfect. He mounted the stage and placed the still covered painting on the chair, then made his way back over to Kaley.

Taking her hand, he led her over to where the painting sat on the stage. "I want you to know I should have realized how much you meant to me long before now. But maybe this will convince you."

He pulled the covering off the painting, and the room gasped. It was Kaley lying on the sofa in the sunroom. He'd painted her in a beautiful nightgown, short, but it covered the important parts. Anthony had captured the sparkle in her eyes, her sensuality, and most of all, her love of animals. Nugget nestled in her arms and a cat was curled in her lap.

"Oh my goodness." Kaley put her hand over her heart. "Anthony."

"I tried my best to capture your essences. Your heart, soul, and kindness, but also how you love animals and take care of everyone."

"It's… Beautiful isn't a strong enough word." Kaley slid to his side.

"I will cherish you the rest of my life, Kaley. I know it's too soon for those types of words, but I can't help them. You're working at overcoming your fear, and there's no reason I can't either."

Her eyes filled with tears. She rose on her toes and kissed him. The group in Wicked Sanctuary started clapping and yelling.

"Do I get that in my gallery?" Dane yelled.

"Maybe." Anthony leaned down. "I have another painting that is just for me."

"Oh?"

"Yes. You nude, reclining on that studio sofa in all your glory."

Her cheeks went red, and he captured her lips again. He was going to marry this woman as soon as he could convince her of it.

EPILOGUE

Kaley pushed the hair away from her face. It had been six months since she and Anthony declared their love for each other. One of the first things he did was insist she move in with him. In a way, she was glad to get out of her small apartment, though it was a little bittersweet. She'd come into her own there. Made her choices and they'd worked. She had a solid business. And love. So much love.

Today Anthony wanted her to meet him downtown not far from Sweet & Savory, but he wouldn't tell her why. When she pulled up to the address, she double-checked it. Yep, this was the address.

She got out of her dog grooming van and stared at the empty store front. Why did he want to meet her here?

"Hey, sweetheart."

She turned to see Anthony walking toward her, a big smile on his face. "Why here?"

"You'll see." He took a set of keys out of his pocket, opened the door, and guided her inside.

She glanced around. This was a very nice place. But Anthony guided her past two swinging doors and into the back. Three huge tubs sat along one wall.

"I don't get it."

"This used to be a self-serve dog wash place."

"Oh." She'd never paid that close of attention. "When did it close?"

"About two years ago. I've talked with the building owner and had everything inspected."

She frowned. "Why?"

"Because this is now going to become Fluff & Puff."

She froze in place as her eyes widened. "What?"

"I saw the empty building two months ago and started making inquiries. It's yours if you want it."

"Anthony." She couldn't find the words. "I don't know if I can afford the rent." While she was doing well, this was a big step.

He slipped his arm around her waist. "It's a present."

She tilted her head up and looked at him. "No. It's too much."

"I know you don't want me spending money on you, but it's my money to spend. Before you say anything, it's not going to hurt my bank account. I've been selling like hot cakes at the gallery, both here and at Dane's other one in Chicago."

"But it's your money."

"It's our money." He turned her to face him. "Since you came into my life, I'm happier; my muse is painting up a storm in my head, and I love you."

She pulled out of his hold and ran her hand over the tub. "It's going to take a lot to get this place functional."

"Just say the word. Zeke and Gabriel said they would get a crew together. Allyson has already checked on permits, and you have intimate ties to an artist who can paint your windows with cute animal pictures."

Kaley laughed and launched herself into his arm. "I love you so much."

"Good." He took a step back.

She frowned as he knelt down, then he held out a box. "Marry me?"

"Oh, hell yeah."

* * * *

Thank you for reading *Edged,* the seventh book in the Wicked Sanctuary series. If you enjoyed this book, please consider leaving a review on Goodreads, or your favorite retailer, and know that it would be greatly appreciated.
For new release information and news about Marie Tuhart, please join her newsletter.
If you enjoyed *Edged, Unmasked* will be released in Winter of 2023. You can pre-order now.

ABOUT THE AUTHOR

Marie Tuhart lives in the beautiful Pacific Northwest. She loves to read and write, and when she's not writing, she spends time with her two dogs, Tommy and Trina, family, traveling and enjoying life.

Marie is a multi-published author with The Wild Rose Press and Trifecta Publishing, and is self-published. To be alerted to her new releases, you can join Marie's newsletter or check out her website: www.mairetuhart.com

And for up-to-date information about releases, please consider joining Marie's mailing list.

OTHER BOOKS BY MARIE TUHART

Claimed by the Sheikh

Billionaire's Cowboy's Conquest

Tempt (Wicked Sanctuary Series)

Entice (Wicked Sanctuary Series)

Seduce (Wicked Sanctuary Series)

Ravish (Wicked Sanctuary Series)

Possess (Wicked Sanctuary Series)

Tantalize (Wicked Sanctuary Series)

Edged (Wicked Sanctuary Series)

Unmasked (Wicked Sanctuary) Fall 2023

Too Hot (Wicked Sanctuary) Spring 2024

Wicked Sanctuary Novella's:

Untamed

Power Play

Claiming Rose

PREVIEW OF *UNMASKED*

Ellie Tanner grinned as Sierra was pulled onto the stage by one of the male strippers. She'd been a little doubtful about having the bachelorette party at The Oasis, but all seemed to be going well. Max Preston, Sierra's fiancé and owner of the local BDSM club apparently hadn't objected.

"Great party," Tessa, one of the bridesmaids, commented.

"I'm glad it's working out."

"We're loving it," Crystal said. She was the other bridesmaid. Both had contacted Ellie and asked her to have the party here. Ellie had done her due diligence and checked the place out, chatted with the owner and made the decision it would be okay. Some might think she was going overboard, but she liked to provide the best experience for her clients that she could.

"Let's dance," one of the other women called out.

Sierra left the stage and joined the women on the dance floor. Ellie couldn't stop smiling as the music grew louder. She started cleaning up the table, throwing away the paper from the presents, penis shaped plates from the cake, kinky presents in bags, and other things.

All in all, this was successful party.

"Come on, Ellie." Regina tugged at her hand to get her out on the dance floor.

"Sorry. I'm the planner, not a guest." This was her standard line. She stood on the sidelines watching the women. She didn't involve herself in her clients' lives any more than necessary, although with Sierra, it was a little harder. In between meetings with her, Crystal, and Tessa about the bachelorette party, she'd also planned Sierra's wedding.

They'd had several get-togethers, at Max and Sierra's home and at the club. Ellie had been curious about Wicked Sanctuary, and Sierra had been gracious enough to show her around and talk with her about the BDSM lifestyle.

Regina opened her mouth. "Oh shit."

"What?" Sierra yelled.

"Turn around," Regina said.

Ellie turned, following Regina's gaze.

"Shit is right," Sierra commented as her eyes grew wide.

"Wow," Ellis said under her breath. She could only stare at the line of men standing shoulder-to-shoulder with their arms crossed over their chests and staring at the group. The men were similarly dressed in jeans and t-shirts, their unwavering gazes on the women. Damn, they looked impressive.

The testosterone and dominance from these men filled the air. A shiver snaked up Ellie's spine. She recognized Max, Jordan, and Damon, but not the rest of the men, although she suspected they were attached to the other women still here at the party. But when she counted men, there was an extra.

From talking to Sage, Ellie was aware Sage was a Domme, so who was he? He stood at the end, but there was something about him that screamed, "I'm in charge". His short dark hair gave off the don't mess with me vibe. Maybe it was the way he stood. Legs apart, arms crossed over chest. Just like the other men. No, it was more than that, because all the guys held the same stance. He only had eyes for her. That was the difference. That and the intensity of his gaze made Ellie's heart flutter. Those dark brown eyes never left her face.

Ellie couldn't glance away. He was a tall man with

wide shoulders. Dressed much like the others in dark clothing. He looked…ferocious wasn't the right word. He didn't look angry or upset, more intrigued than anything.

Her breath caught in her throat and her lady parts started to tingle. That hadn't happened in a long, long time. What the hell was wrong with her?

The club had gone silent, the music shut off, and the male strippers melted away. Ellie blinked as one by one, the men marched to their respective women. Except him. He stood staring at her.

She forced herself to turn away and finished packing up the presents, with help from Sage, who seemed to want to steer as clear of the men as Ellie did.

"Who planned this?" Damon asked.

"That was me." Ellie turned to face Damon.

"You're the wedding planner," Max stated.

"Obviously," she muttered.

"Party planner as well," Sierra said. "Don't pick on Ellie."

"I'm not." Max shook his head. "Ellie surprised me, that's all."

Sage coughed. "We've got the presents packed up. Max, if you give me your keys, Ellie and I will load them while you finish sorting this out."

"Sure." Max tossed his keys to Sage.

Together they gathered up the gifts and headed out. The man staring at Ellie took a step, but stopped when Sage glared at him. He held his hands up and backed away.

"That was impressive," Ellie said.

"You just need to know how to handle the Doms."

Ellie loaded the gifts while Sage ran back inside and picked up the leftover cake. "I'm heading out. Will you give Max his keys?" Sage said, dropping them in Ellie's palm.

"Sure. 'Night, Sage." Locking the SUV, Ellie waked back inside and joined Max and Sierra. "Everything is in the car." She held the keys out to Max. "Sage took off."

Ellie turned to Sierra. "The cake needs to go into the fridge when you get home."

"I'll make sure it does." Sierra's words were slightly slurred.

How much had Sierra had to drink? Ellie wasn't sure.

"No, I'll make sure," Max said.

"Thank you, Ellie. It was a great party." Sierra hugged her, then stepped back.

"Logan," Max called out. "Can you escort Ellie home, please?"

The man who'd been staring at her joined them. "It would be my pleasure."

"I'm fine. I didn't drink and can easily get a rideshare."

"Unacceptable," Logan declared.

Ellie rolled her eyes.

"Come on, Miss Party Planner. I'll get you home." He placed his hand under her elbow.

A spark went through Ellie's body at his touch. She allowed him to escort her out of the building. "This isn't necessary, you know." Ellie wasn't sure she wanted to be alone with the obviously dominant male.

He glanced at her. "It is." He led her to a big black SUV. "You need a ride home, and I want to make sure you get there safely."

What was it with men and their big vehicles? Ellie wasn't short by any means, but even she would need the running board to get inside this thing.

The lights flashed and the horn beeped as he

unlocked it. She reached for the door handle, but he had it open before she could touch it.

"Thank you." It was nice for a man to be a gentleman. She gazed up and judged how to get into the vehicle without having her dress ride up and showing off her underwear. There was a handhold right inside the door. Taking a step up onto the running board and she reached for the handhold.

"Easy." His deep voice was right next to Ellie's ear as his hands snuck around her waist and he lifted her into the cab.

Ellie squealed. "I was fine getting in by myself." This man was taking liberties since they'd just met.

A grin played around his lips. Those full, sensual lips. "I'm sure you could, but it was easier for both of us this way." He stepped back, his gaze lingering on her legs before he pushed the door shut.

Ellie blew out a breath and did up her seatbelt. The heat of his gaze on her legs filled her body with unwanted desire. *Don't let him get to you.* Logan climbed into the vehicle with cat-like grace and started the engine. "Where to?"

"Fourteen sixty-three Middleton Court."

"Got it." He pulled out of the parking lot. "I'm Logan Wolfe, by the way."

"Ellie Tanner."

"I know." He flashed Ellie a grin, and her lady parts tingled once again. She barely stopped her eyes from rolling.

"How do you know?" she asked.

"I saw you walking around the club with Sierra."

Of course. He was one of the club members. All of the men tonight were members of Wicked Sanctuary. Ellie shifted in her seat. Would she see him in the club if she joined? Ellie had an appointment with Max in two weeks.

She was surprised when they made it to her apartment so quickly and easily. Well, it was after midnight and traffic was light. Logan parked the vehicle at the front, near the entrance. "Wait and I'll help you out."

She opened her mouth to tell him there was no need, but the look in his eyes made her swallow her words. Ellie nodded. Was this what Sierra meant when she said the Doms used silent communication?

While he walked around the vehicle, she unbuckled her seatbelt and took a deep breath. The door opened and she turned. Hands framed her waist and lifted her out. Her knees were slightly weak when her feet touched the ground. Why was his touch doing this to her?

"Thank you." She moved out of his hold, not liking

how her body reacted. As good-looking as Logan was, she didn't have time for a man in her life. She also wasn't sure at all about the lifestyle he lived.

"I'll walk you in." He pushed the door shut and locked the vehicle.

"You…" Her words trailed off when he looked at her. That stare. "Fine." She huffed and walked down the sidewalk to the lobby door. She punched in the code and the door clicked. "There. I'm in."

Reaching around her, he pushed the door open and gestured for her to enter. Tiredness crept into her bones and she didn't have the energy left to argue with him. Ellie marched to the elevator and punched the button. When it arrived, he stepped into the small enclosure with her.

Leather and…she couldn't quite identify his scent. Ellie kept her gaze on the elevator door. Logan, for some reason, made her feel small and feminine. That was so not her. She wasn't a fragile woman.

Finally, the door opened on the tenth floor and Ellie quickly made her way to her apartment. "Thank you. Have a good rest of your evening." She put the key in the lock.

"I need to look around."

She'd heard from the other women how protective their men were, but this was pushing her buttons. "There's no need."

"There is every need." He pushed her away and opened her door.

"Enough." Ellie stepped in front of him and lifted her chin. "I allowed you to accompany me this far; you are not going to enter my home. End of discussion. If you persist, I will call the police. We can end this encounter on friendly terms or as adversaries. Your choice."

He stared at her and she stared right back. "I'm on the tenth floor of a secured building," she felt compelled to add.

"Doesn't mean someone can't get in." His brown eyes blazed with…anger? No. Something else. "You are a stubborn woman."

"You better believe it." She tilted her head back to meet his gaze. "Thank you for the escort, Logan. I appreciated the gesture. Good night." She gestured to the hallway.

He didn't move. For a moment, his eyes flared with fire, then it was gone. "Good night, Ellie. I'll see you another time. Lock up after me." He reached up and ran his finger over her cheek, then he turned and sauntered back to the elevator.

Ellie shut the door and threw the deadbolt as fire ran over her skin from his touch. *No, no, no.* She was so not going down this road. She didn't need a man in her life.

A giggle left her lips. She and Sierra had talked about Ellie joining Wicked Sanctuary. Wasn't that what joining the club was about? She shook her head. No, that was about releasing tensions, not about finding a man. She'd talked with both Sierra and Crystal. The club would give her a chance to explore a side of herself she'd always been curious about. That's all it was. With a sigh, she pulled away from the door and headed for her bedroom.

One thing she did know, she'd stay clear of Logan in the club. The man was too intense. Too serious. She wanted to have some fun, not be ordered around.

Another shiver raced through her as she thought about Logan's commanding air and penetrating gaze. She didn't want intense.

Right?

www.ingramcontent.com/pod-product-compliance
Lightning Source LLC
Chambersburg PA
CBHW061248210726
48293CB00003B/902